CITY
OF THE
FUTURE

Written by Matt Thomas
Designed by Tracey Cunnell
Edited by Pat Hegarty
Illustrated by Rob Davis

Cover background © iStockphoto

Created by WizzBook Ltd
Copyright © 2009 WizzBook Ltd
All rights reserved

First published in the UK
by Potter Books, RH17 5PA, UK

www.potterbooks.co.uk

Printed in the UK
by CPI Bookmarque,
Croydon, CRO 4TD

CITY
OF THE
FUTURE

Matt Thomas

Illustrated by Rob Davis

WHAT HAPPENS NEXT? YOU DECIDE...

The M.I.Five is about to embark on its second
top secret mission. Last time the story focused
on Jake, the maths whizz, but this time round it's
super-intelligent Sarah's turn. On four occasions
you'll be prompted to choose from a selection
of alternative chapters, and your choice will
determine how the plot unfolds.

1
a new Home

Sarah Moore sat alone in the back of a chauffeur-driven car, as it crawled past some of London's most famous landmarks. It was eight-thirty in the morning and, as usual, the traffic was bad. Sarah didn't mind though, it gave her a chance to have a closer look at the city. London was full of interesting buildings and people, thought Sarah, but outside on the crowded streets no one seemed to notice.

In some ways Sarah was just a normal girl. Like any twelve year-old, she liked films, books, going shopping, hanging out with her friends and she had a secret soft spot for TV soaps. Best of all, she loved curling up with a magazine full of fashion tips and hot gossip about celebrities. However, there was another side to Sarah; one that was less ordinary. It was the side that could speak seven languages. fluently, that played the piano and guitar at grade eight and passed eleven GCSEs at the age of nine. Sarah was able to do all this, firstly, because she'd worked exceptionally hard, but secondly because she was incredibly clever – in fact, she was a genius.

Her exceptional intelligence wasn't the only thing that set Sarah apart from normal girls. Her life was pretty extraordinary. Sarah was on her way back from one of her regular meetings with Jonathan Holmes, the British Prime Minister. It still seemed incredible to Sarah that the most powerful man in the country wanted her opinion on top secret matters of vital importance to the country. After all, how many twelve year-olds do you know who can say that?

"Here we are, Agent Moore," said the driver.

"Thank you, Charlie," said Sarah, stepping out of the car and hopping up the steps of the anonymous building on the north bank of the River Thames. It was here that Sarah lived and worked. She didn't go to school any more, at least not in the traditional sense. Sarah pressed her finger against the biometric lock and the door swung open.

As she stepped into the entrance hall, a computerised voice said, "Good morning, Agent Moore."

Sarah hurried down the stark, white hallway, whistling a song to herself as she went. From the outside, the building looked like a normal office, but Sarah had just entered the Government's Secret Intelligence Agency, or MI6 as it is more commonly known. Believe it or not, Sarah was a secret agent, working as part of the new children's division – her and four of her friends. The division had several boring, official names, but to most people in MI6 they were known simply as the 'M.I.Five', the M.I. bit being short for Mega Intelligent.

Ordinarily, because a secret agent's work is extremely dangerous, MI6 isn't in the habit of employing children. However, in the case of Sarah and her friends, they had made an exception. The reason for their special treatment was simple; three months ago this incredible bunch of young people had saved the world. A dangerous madman named Jean-Paul Laurent had come very close to starting World War III. Sarah and her friends had discovered his plan and managed to stop him. The government, whilst a little embarrassed not to have uncovered the plot themselves, were very grateful to the kids and only too happy to have them working to stop such a thing ever happening again.

Sarah hopped up a flight of stairs to the breakfast

room where she found Jake looking bleary-eyed as he forced down a bowl of cereal.

"Hey, Sarah..." mumbled Jake, stifling a big yawn.

"Morning, Jake," replied Sarah, grabbing a piece of fruit. Jake was a maths genius, as well as being one of the bravest boys Sarah had ever met, but he certainly wasn't a morning person. "Looking forward to the demo?" she asked.

The demo she was talking about had been organised by the kids' scientist, Alex. He had been holed up in his new lab for the best part of a month and today he was going to unveil his new inventions. The kids had been looking forward to it for ages.

"Can't wait," replied Jake.

"Neither can I," said Sarah, as she checked her watch and flicked on the TV. The morning news was on. A reporter was standing outside the front door of 10 Downing Street reporting back to the studio.

"It's a very important week for Britain. The government is set to make the Future Cities decision and all eyes are on Downing Street..." proclaimed the reporter, as Sarah furrowed her brow with concern. This was what the Prime Minister had discussed with her this morning.

The Future Cities project was an ambitious building programme to construct a series of new cities across Britain. It would provide thousands of badly-needed homes for people and everyone thought it was a great idea. The only problem was that the government couldn't make up its mind about who would build them. Obviously, whoever got the contract would make billions of pounds in profit, so competition for the job had been fierce. The applicants had been whittled down to Heron Construction, a rapidly growing company owned by a charismatic billionaire called Rufus Heron, and Clean Air Co., a much smaller company run by an architect called Sir Brian Wilkins.

This morning the Prime Minister had told Sarah that the majority of his cabinet was leaning towards awarding the contract to Heron Construction. The problem was that Jonathan wasn't sure that he could trust Heron. He wasn't sure why, but something about him made Jonathan feel very uneasy.

Just as Sarah was thinking about him, Heron appeared on the TV screen. "And here's Rufus Heron to give us an exclusive interview," announced the reporter, as the camera pulled back to reveal a well-groomed man in his forties. "Mr Heron, how does it feel to be so close to winning the contract to build these innovative cities?"

"I'm absolutely delighted. Heron Construction is the perfect choice."

As Heron continued, Sarah began to agree more and more with the Prime Minister. She couldn't put her finger on it, but there was something odd about him.

"What's up, Sarah?" asked Jake. Even in his state

of half-consciousness, he could see something was bothering her.

"Probably nothing," muttered Sarah, as much to herself as to Jake. "Come on, let's go. We'll pick up Chun Mai on the way," she added, as she flicked off the TV.

"Where is she?" asked Jake.

"Where do you think?" replied Sarah, grinning.

Chun Mai was the group's computer expert. At ten years old she was already one of the world's best computer hackers – there was very little she couldn't find out with a computer and an internet connection. When the kids joined MI6 she had been given a huge room full of powerful computers to play with. She couldn't have been happier with this arrangement and spent most of her days joyfully tapping away. She'd occasionally try to explain to the other kids what she was doing, but she soon lost them. Even Alex, the science whizz, had only a vague idea what she was talking about most of the time.

When Jake and Sarah walked in, Chun Mai was staring intently at her bank of computer screens, tapping two keyboards at once. She jumped with fright when she saw them, quickly pressing a button that made all the screens go blank.

"Oh, err, hi guys," she said, trying to sound casual.

"What are you up to Chun Mai?" asked Sarah, suspiciously.

"Nothing," replied Chun Mai innocently, attempting to avoid Sarah's gaze.

"C'mon Chun Mai. We know you well enough to tell when you're hiding something," laughed Jake. "And you always tap your foot like that when you're nervous," he added, pointing.

Chun Mai looked at the floor bashfully. "Okay, I'm kind-a messing about with NASA's computer."

"NASA?" said Sarah, shocked. "As in NASA the American Aeronautics and Space Administration?"

"Yep," replied Chun Mai, guiltily.

"Blimey, Chun Mai! Why?" exclaimed Jake.

"To see if I can, mainly," said Chun Mai.

"And...?" asked Sarah.

"See for yourself," replied Chun Mai, turning her screens back on to reveal various pictures of rockets and documents with NASA logos on them. Chun Mai continued typing. "I suppose you guys are on your way to Alex's meeting, right?" she said, as Jake and Sarah looked at each other in shock. "I'll come with you. Just let me send a message to these NASA guys. They really should know that their computers aren't as secure as they thought."

"Chun Mai, are you the best computer hacker in the world?" asked Jake.

"I'm not sure about that, Jake," said Chun Mai, hitting 'Enter'. "But I'm certainly better than whoever designed NASA's system."

Alex's lab was vast and messy, with blueprints covering every wall and half-finished robots sitting in tangled heaps on the tables. Strange and wonderful noises filled the air and, at fairly regular intervals, something blew up. It was by far the most impressive part of the kids' operation. As well as his dream lab, MI6 had also given Alex a team of ten scientists to command. It meant that he could work on ten times as many inventions and Alex was in absolute heaven!

When the kids entered, Alex was hunched over a small but complicated-looking robot, screwdriver in hand, as his team bustled around him, building and maintaining his weird and wonderful machines.

"Hi guys!" he said. "You're just in time!"

Alex closed the lid of the machine he was tinkering with and switched it on. "Who wants a cup of tea?" he asked. The kids all nodded, more out of curiosity than thirst.

"Four cups of tea please, House-Bot," commanded Alex. The small robot took flight and whizzed silently across the lab to the kitchen area. Long metallic tentacles emerged from the robot and picked up the kettle and a bottle of milk. Alex turned proudly to face the kids. "He's a personal project of mine," he said. "He can perform over a hundred household tasks – it's going to revolutionise..." Alex tailed off as he heard an almighty clang. House-Bot had dropped the kettle on the floor and was in the process of pouring milk on to a computer keyboard.

"Obviously there are still a few bugs to be ironed out," he said as House-Bot's tentacles began to spin wildly in the air, knocking over a tray of teacups. Alex's assistants tried to deactivate the robot, but it was too late. Suddenly House-Bot turned towards Alex and began to emit a high-pitched beeping sound. Alex knew what that meant. "Everybody get down – NOW!" he shouted, as the beeping grew louder. Seconds later – BANG! It exploded, sending mechanical parts flying everywhere, shattering most of the lab's windows.

Once the smoking springs, circuit boards and bits of metal casing had all come to rest, Alex stood up.

"Is everyone okay?" he shouted. Hearing vague murmurs from the kids and his staff, Alex breathed a sigh of relief. He picked up a part of the shattered robot and shook his head. "He's the third one this week," he said, looking down at the singed, broken mess. "Why do you keep exploding?" he sighed.

"What's going on here?" boomed a familiar voice from the doorway. It was Robert, the final member of the team. He was tanned and dressed in a white suit and sunglasses. "Honestly, I go away for five minutes and the whole place falls apart," he added.

The kids jumped up off the floor and ran over to greet him. Robert was a world-famous magician despite being only twelve years old. He'd just returned from a global tour that had seen him perform for some of the world's most influential people.

"Hey, Roberto, how was the tour?" asked Alex, grinning at his friend.

"Great," he replied. "In fact, it was such a success that I might change my name. I need something a bit grander, now that I'm so popular. Maybe 'The Great and Ravishing Roberto, Magician Extraordinaire!'"

Sarah rolled her eyes. All the kids liked Robert, but he could be a real bighead sometimes. All the attention his magic show had been getting recently would only make him worse.

"Shall we get going?" asked Sarah, before Robert could start bragging about all the places he'd been to.

"We have to wait for Julian," sighed Alex.

The rest of the group groaned. Julian was their 'handler'. Despite their heroism in catching Jean-Paul Laurent, a few people at MI6 still didn't think that children could cope with dangerous government work. So MI6 had put Julian Morris in charge of the M.I.Five. He was a very clever man and a first-class agent, but he just couldn't get his head around the fact that children were working as spies. So far, all he'd really managed to do was get in their way.

Just at that moment, Julian walked in. He was a large man with grey hair and bushy eyebrows that knitted into a frown when he was being serious – which was almost always. He was a stickler for the rules and believed in efficiency and discipline at all times. "I haven't got much time," he barked. "I'm expecting a call from the Deputy PM. Alex, what have you got?"

"I think you'll like what you see, Julian," Alex said.

"It's Agent Morris if you don't mind, Alex," said Julian, irritably.

"Right you are, sorry Agent Morris," said Alex. "The first thing I wanted to show you was this..."

With that, Alex pulled a small mouse out of his pocket and placed it on the table. The mouse immediately began running round and round, chasing its own tail.

"Why on earth are you showing me a mouse?" asked Julian.

"It's not a mouse, Agent Morris. Well, not a real one anyway," said Alex, pulling a remote control out of his pocket. He pressed the pause button and the mouse froze in its tracks. Then, using a small joystick on the side of the remote, Alex started manoeuvring the mouse before making it jump back on to his hand.

"That's amazing, Alex!" said Chun Mai. The rest of the kids agreed, but Julian was still frowning.

"Very impressive," said Julian, "But may I ask why you've spent MI6 money on a remote controlled mouse? What possible use does it have?" he added, peering sternly over his spectacles.

Alex grinned, tugged the mouse's tail and "What possible use does it have?" echoed from a speaker. It was a perfect recording of Julian's last sentence. The kids grinned at each other as Julian shifted uncomfortably.

"It's a bug," said Alex. "It can be operated by remote control from up to fifty miles away."

"And mice can squeeze into the tiniest spaces..." said Jake.

"Exactly," said Alex. "Now we can listen in on almost any conversation."

"That's absolutely brilliant, Alex," said Sarah. "Anything else?"

"Of course! Actually, you'll like this one, Sarah,"

17

said Alex, producing five small devices that looked like MP3 players. "These are auto-translators," he said, proudly. "Remind me, what languages do you speak?" he asked.

"Umm, Mandarin, Japanese, Spanish, German, French and Russian. Oh, and some Swahili," said Sarah, proudly.

"Right, we'll use that as the example," said Alex. He said the word, "Swahili," into the auto-translator, followed by, "Hello, Sarah, how are you?"

The machine clicked and whirred for a moment before, out of the speaker, came the words, "Jambo, Sarah, habari?" Sarah stared at the box, then at Alex, completely awestruck.

"Is that right, Sarah?" asked Alex.

"Yes. Even the accent's perfect," said Sarah picking up an auto-translator and staring at it, amazed.

"Thought so. It can translate with one hundred per cent accuracy into over a hundred languages," said Alex, handing each of the kids a translator. "Right! Now it's time for the grand finale. Follow me, guys!"

They followed Alex on to the roof to the entrance of the hoverpod hangar. The hoverpods were about the size of a small car and Alex's favourite invention to date. They were compact flying machines that changed colour to blend in with their surroundings, so they were almost invisible to the naked eye. They weren't a new invention, but Alex had made some

18

interesting changes since they'd last been used and he was keen to show his friends the results. He ran his finger across the security lock of the hangar and opened the door. Inside, two hoverpods were covered with a large dust sheet. With a dramatic flourish, Alex pulled the sheet away.

"Let me introduce you to the next generation of hoverpod, Bertha and Betty," said Alex, standing in front of two brand new, highly-modified models. The kids gasped. The hoverpods were so sleek and shiny! The old ones had been cobbled together from scrap and had looked amateurish, but these gleaming machines looked like something from the future.

"Not only can these hoverpods handle top speed more comfortably..." began Alex.

"That's a relief," said Jake, wincing as he remembered his disastrous hoverpod race.

"They are now capable of travelling underwater," continued Alex. A murmur passed through the entire group. Even Julian looked impressed.

"And that's not all," said Alex. "You know how you guys say I like my gadgets? Well, check this out."

Alex whipped out another remote control and began pressing buttons. One of the hoverpods whirred into life and rose slowly off the tarmac.

"The hoverpod now has remote control," said Alex triumphantly, manoeuvring the hoverpod gently from side-to-side in mid-air.

The kids were amazed and gave Alex a round of applause. Alex grinned awkwardly back at them and took a bow. Unfortunately, in his excitement he dropped the remote. Suddenly, one of the hoverpods roared into life and started racing towards them.

They all threw themselves to the ground as it skimmed over their heads and crashed into the back wall of the hangar with an almighty bang!

As debris rained down around them, the kids slowly got to their feet and shook the dust from their hair. They looked at Alex in disbelief; the boy was probably one of the greatest inventors in the world, but he wasn't half clumsy.

"Can I just point out that that's the second time you've almost killed us today Alex," said Jake.

Demonstration day was always dangerous!

2

future cities

It was early evening. Down at M.I.Five HQ, Alex was busy putting the smashed hoverpod back together, Jake was playing Sudoku, Robert was practising card tricks and Chun Mai was doing goodness knows what in the computer room.

Sarah, however, was getting ready to go out. At their last meeting, the Prime Minister had invited her to a party. Well, it wasn't so much a party as a competition – with the deadline for the Future Cities decision approaching, the government had asked Rufus Heron and Sir Brian Wilkins to present their final plans. The presentations would take place at Banqueting House in front of the government and other VIPs. Sarah was glad to be going. Firstly, because it would give her an opportunity to see whether her suspicions about Rufus Heron were really justified, and secondly, because it gave her the chance to dress up for once.

Unlike Chun Mai, who barely ever changed out of her jeans and hoodie, Sarah loved girly clothes. She had spent ages choosing the perfect outfit, finally settling on a pink skirt and top with matching bag and shoes. As Sarah twirled in front of the mirror she was almost giddy with excitement. For a fleeting moment she felt like a normal girl, but then the intercom in her room buzzed sharply and Sarah was snapped out of her daydream with a jolt.

"Agent Moore, your car has arrived," intoned a tinny voice over the intercom.

At Banqueting House, Sarah took a moment to admire the spectacular building and then followed the chattering party-goers inside. With a slight look of surprise, an attendant took her invitation and opened the doors to the great hall. Everywhere she looked, people stood chatting in small groups as waiters flitted between them with silver trays piled high with finger food. Sarah soon spotted four or five members of the British government and several European presidents and prime ministers. Jonathan Holmes noticed her across the room and nodded a greeting, but it was obvious that he was deep in conversation with a group of very grave-looking men, so Sarah decided not to bother him.

Sarah took a glass of orange juice from a tray and continued to look around. A stage had been built at the far end, in front of which were ten rows of chairs.

A busy-looking lady with a head-set and clipboard walked on to the stage and tapped the microphone to check that it was on.

"Ladies and gentlemen, if you would like to take your seats, the presentations will begin shortly."

As soon as everyone was seated, the lights dimmed and the room was plunged into darkness. It was very effective – the crowd stopped talking and all eyes were on the stage. Suddenly, spotlights swept across the room and dancers strutted on to the stage as loud music began booming out from the speakers.

The words 'WELCOME TO THE FUTURE' appeared on a screen at the back of the stage and, as the music came to its dramatic end, a large firework went off, surrounded by bursts of dry ice from a hidden smoke machine.

The whole thing was like a West End show, thought Sarah. Robert would have loved it. As the smoke cleared, a figure emerged. It was Rufus Heron. He paused to enjoy the thunderous applause, then slowly approached the microphone.

"Ladies and gentlemen, good evening and welcome!" he proclaimed, with his head held high.

The crowd responded by clapping even more enthusiastically. These were serious and important people who were not easily impressed, but Rufus Heron had whipped them into a frenzy!

"Tonight, I will show you the future," Heron said, the crowd hanging on his every word. "With these new cities, Heron Construction will change the world."

Heron certainly is charismatic, thought Sarah. She was almost carried away by his stage presence, along with the rest of the crowd.

He continued talking as a slick presentation of Heron Construction's plans flashed up on the screen behind him. The cities were very futuristic – with shiny steel and glass everywhere, they looked like something from a sci-fi film. Impressive, but a little flashy, thought Sarah, as she stared at the vast stadiums, skyscrapers and shopping malls. It was the environmental impact that worried Sarah most. The cities were all surrounded by giant motorways and there was no mention of renewable energy at all. It appeared that Rufus Heron was planning to power these cities by traditional methods like coal or oil that polluted the atmosphere and contributed to global warming. That was the last thing Britain needed.

Heron moved seamlessly to the front of the stage as he built to his big finish. "Heron cities are the right choice, the only choice," he proclaimed. "I guarantee to build bigger, better cities than Clean Air Co. is offering...for half the price!"

That made Sarah sit up and take notice. It simply couldn't be true, could it? 'Bigger, better' cities for less money? It just didn't make sense. She looked over to the Prime Minister, who was shaking his head; he didn't buy it either. Unfortunately, the rest of the crowd seemed to have been entirely sucked in by Heron's assured presentation.

"Our future – Britain's future – is in your hands, ladies and gentlemen" said Heron, smoothly, as the crowd applauded enthusiastically. Sarah sat stony-faced as she watched Rufus Heron leave the stage to shake hands with various VIPs. He clearly thought that the contract was as good as his. Half the price, she thought. How could that be possible?

The lady with the head-set and clipboard returned to the stage. "Our second presentation this evening will be given by Sir Brian Wilkins," she announced, desperately trying to regain the audience's attention.

There was a small ripple of applause as Sir Brian climbed on to the stage with not so much as a note of music to herald his arrival. The audience was already becoming restless as they began to realise that Sir Brian's presentation wasn't going to be as flashy and grand as Heron's.

"Err...good evening, everyone," began Sir Brian, meekly. He was a short, thin man with thick-lensed spectacles, and was clearly not used to speaking in public. He read from a set of cards, barely looking up at the audience. Occasionally, he stopped to press a key on his laptop to show technical drawings of his cities on a screen behind him. After the flamboyant spectacle that was Heron's presentation, he simply didn't stand a chance. Before very long, people were fidgeting and checking their watches. Nobody was listening – except for Sarah and the Prime Minister.

Sir Brian wasn't particularly engaging as a speaker, but his ideas were fascinating. He had a plan to build cities that would be entirely powered by renewable energy; there would be no cars on the roads – and everyone would travel by electric tram. They would be the first completely environmentally-friendly cities in the world. There would be plenty of parks and playing fields, and the houses would be affordable so that anyone could move there – not just the rich.

If Sarah had had a vote it would have gone to Sir Brian. His cities sounded like great places to live. It was just too bad that no one was listening to him. The lady next to Sarah stifled a yawn. Sarah glanced over her shoulder and noticed Heron at the back of the room chatting and shaking hands with some people who had stood up before the end of Sir Brian's speech. How rude, thought Sarah.

"Thank you," said Sir Brian, as his speech drew to a close. There was a very brief, subdued round of applause as people sprang to their feet, delighted that his speech was over. As the crowd headed to the back of the room to try to speak to Rufus Heron, a dejected Sir Brian slowly left the stage. He already knew that he was a beaten man.

Sarah sighed with sympathy and regret as she watched the unappreciated architect slip away, and then glanced across the room to Rufus Heron, who was looking very pleased with himself, as he chatted to the crowd of people that had gathered around him. Tonight had only intensified Sarah's feelings of distrust. Something was definitely up, but she still couldn't put her finger on exactly what it was.

The only other person in the room, maybe in the world, who didn't trust Rufus Heron was currently standing across the hall with his brow furrowed in concern. The speeches had left the Prime Minister in a bad mood. He was angry at the lack of interest in Sir Brian's presentation. Aside from his personal feelings about Heron, he genuinely believed that Sir Brian's cities would be better for the country. How was he going to convince everyone else of that after Heron's assured performance tonight?

Just then, Heron approached, smiling broadly. He strode over to the Prime Minister and shook him warmly by the hand as if they were old buddies when, in fact, they had only met a couple of times.

"Prime Minister, I'm so glad you could join me tonight," said Heron.

"I arranged the event, Rufus, I couldn't very well not attend," replied Jonathan, coolly.

"Yes, yes, of course. I take it we can count on your support after my presentation?" asked Heron.

"I am yet to make my final decision," snapped Jonathan, dismissively.

Heron smiled thinly. "Prime Minister, I wonder if we might have a word in private?"

This was the last thing that Jonathan wanted but, unable to think of a good reason to refuse the request, he was forced to nod reluctantly. He was beginning to really dislike Heron.

Jonathan led Heron to a small room outside the main hall. As soon as they were inside, Heron began to speak. "I'll get straight to the point, Prime Minister."

"Please do," sighed Jonathan, impatiently.

"You don't like me, that much is obvious. But business is business and I think today has proved beyond any shadow of a doubt that Heron Construction is the best company for the job." Heron offered his hand to the Prime Minister, "So, why don't we just put our differences aside, for the sake of this great country, and start work on these Future Cities?"

Jonathan looked at Heron's hand for a long time. Finally, he spoke. "I'm afraid I can't do that, Rufus."

"Why not?" asked Heron, incredulously.

"I think Sir Brian's plans are better for the country," said Jonathan, waving his hands in the air.

"What?" said Heron, chuckling a little.

"For one thing, they'll be better for the environment. Your cities would be full of smog within weeks!"

Heron smiled icily, "With respect, Prime Minister, practically the whole government supports my plans."

"Well, I don't!" retorted Jonathan, angrily.

Heron could see that this approach wasn't going to get Jonathan on side. He decided to change his tactics. "Prime Minister," he said, smoothly. "I am a very wealthy man, as you know, and most people come round to my way of thinking, with the right amount of…persuasion," he said, raising an eyebrow suggestively.

Jonathan's face reddened and his eyes flashed with anger. "Are you offering me a bribe, Heron?"

"Absolutely not," said Heron, calmly.

"This meeting is over," snapped the Prime Minister, as he headed for the door.

"I'm afraid you can't stand in my way, Prime Minister!" declared Rufus.

Jonathan paused in the doorway and glared back at Rufus, "Maybe not for ever, but I can slow you down. I promise you, Heron, you won't build your cities while I'm Prime Minister!" With that, Jonathan left, slamming the door behind him.

Heron sat down in an old leather armchair and flicked open his mobile. Moments later, the door swung open and a tall, thin, sinister-looking man walked into the room. It was Seymore Snidley, Heron's assistant. "How can I help, Sir?" asked Snidley in his quiet, creepy voice.

"Get Henry down here," said Heron. "We're switching to plan B."

Snidley nodded, "Right away, Sir."

Sarah watched with interest as the Prime Minister stormed out of the room and exited the building, accompanied by his team of security guards and assistants. Shortly afterwards, Heron appeared from the same room with a tall, thin man whom she assumed worked for him. Heron swiftly resumed chatting with the guests and appeared relaxed and friendly. But even from the other side of the room, Sarah could see that he was clenching his fists. He was definitely angry about something, she thought.

The meeting with Jonathan must have gone badly.

As the evening wore on, Sarah continued to keep an eye on Heron. After a while, his skinny employee approached him and whispered something in his ear. Heron politely, but quickly, made his apologies and left with his sidekick.

Sarah knew that she had to follow him. Her instincts told her that something wasn't right about any of this. Heron was up to something. Carefully, she followed the pair along the corridors and out through a back door. Finding herself in a dingy car park behind the kitchens, she quickly crouched down behind a bin. Peering out, she watched as they approached two burly bodyguards and a bald man, who were waiting for them by two black limos. The bald man had his back to Sarah which made it hard to hear what he was saying, but from Heron's response she was sure it was something about money.

"No, Henry, two million or I'll find someone else..." said Heron, quietly. The bald man shrugged and began to respond, but Snidley cut him off.

"Sir, if I may..."

"What is it, Snidley?" asked Heron, turning to face his assistant.

"In view of the time-sensitive nature of the job, not to mention the considerable amount of money we'll be making, perhaps a small bonus would be... appropriate," he suggested.

33

"Very well. You can expect an extra half a million upon completion, Henry. Subject to my outright satisfaction, of course," said Heron.

"I'm glad we've come to an arrangement, Rufus," said the bald man. "You know I'm the only one who can do this job on the Prime Minister."

"I suggest you learn to keep your mouth shut, Henry," warned Heron. "Now that's settled, it's time to pay our good friend Jonathan a visit. Come on, let's get going."

Sarah wondered why they were going to see the Prime Minister at this time of night. It was far too late for a meeting and what was this 'job' that the bald man had talked about? A cold chill ran through her. At first, she had thought she was just listening to a boring business conversation. Now, however, it seemed as if they were planning something to do with the Prime Minister, and whatever it was, it didn't sound good. She had to get back and tell the others, quickly.

Snidley and the bald man climbed into one of the limos. Heron was about to do the same himself when he paused and glanced over towards the bins. Sarah noticed with horror that part of her skirt was caught on the bin.

"Who's there?" called Heron, sharply.

Sarah sprang up and tried to run, but in her fancy heels she didn't get far before the bodyguards grabbed her. A thick palm was clasped across her mouth before she could scream. She kicked hard but, against the combined force of two men, she didn't stand a chance. They dragged her over to Heron.

When he saw Sarah he gave her a thin smile. "Isn't it past your bedtime, little girl?"

Sarah simply glared back at Heron with pure hatred; she was absolutely petrified but there was no way she'd let him see that.

"She knows too much. Take her with you," said Heron to his bodyguards. "You know what to do," he added darkly, before getting into his car.

Sarah could just see Heron's limo driving away as she was handcuffed and forced into the back of the other limo. As the locks on the car clicked shut, one of the guards turned round to face her through the small window at the front of the limo.

"Don't even think about moving," he said over the limo's intercom.

Sarah nodded. But as they set off, she slowly and subtly tapped a button on her watch. A red light began to blink.

3
Hoverpod rescue

Jake sat slumped on the couch in the lounge at HQ watching the closing stages of a football match. He yawned. The game wasn't important or particularly interesting. He let his eyes wander over to Robert, who was sitting on the other side of the room. He was paying even less attention to the game, as he shuffled a deck of cards with one hand and held a book with the other.

Jake was thinking about going to bed when the peace was shattered. A high-pitched buzzing filled the air and a red light flashed in the corner of the room. A distress beacon had been triggered! Jake and Robert leapt up and dashed downstairs to the crisis room.

The crisis room was a large meeting room with a huge computer screen at one end. Jake and Robert rushed into the room to find Chun Mai and Alex already waiting for them. They were staring at the computer screen with serious looks on their faces, clearly not liking what they were seeing.

"What's going on?" said Jake.

"The distress beacon on Sarah's watch has been triggered," said Chun Mai, gesturing to the computer screen. It showed a small red dot moving across a map of London.

"She must be in a car. She's travelling too quickly to be on foot," frowned Alex.

"So she's been kidnapped?" asked Robert.

"That's the only explanation," muttered Alex. "But how? She was at a party with most of the government and loads of VIPs. The place would've been crawling with security."

"Let's worry about that later," said Jake, taking charge. "We've got to save her! Come on, Robert, we'll take the hoverpod. You two give us tech-support from the computer room."

"One moment please, Jake," came a voice from the giant screen at the end of the room. It was Julian. He had patched into the crisis room from his house.

"Charging in without a plan can be dangerous," he warned, his stern face and eyebrows taking up most of the screen as Sarah's tracking beacon raced further and further away on the other half. "Stay there until I have a concrete plan in place."

"We know what the rule book says, Agent Morris," huffed Jake, impatiently. "But we don't know who has

Sarah or where they're taking her, so there might not be time…"

"My decision is final, Jake!" barked Julian. "I'm in command and I say we wait. Now, Chun Mai what's going on?"

Chun Mai opened her mouth to speak, but Jake interrupted. "There's no time to wait, Julian, can't you see that?"

"I don't like your tone, young man," replied Julian.

"I don't care!" shouted Jake. He turned to face the rest of the kids. "I'm going to save Sarah – alone if I have to!" With that, Jake turned on his heel and strode out of the room.

Without a moment's hesitation, Robert followed Jake.

"Jake...Robert...I'm warning you two. Come back here this instant!" shouted Julian.

"Well, I guess we'd better help them. Otherwise they'll probably get themselves killed," said Chun Mai to Alex as she hurried out of the room.

"Alex, I am ordering you to stay where you are," said Julian, his face scarlet with rage.

"Sorry, Agent Morris," shrugged Alex, as he followed Chun Mai out of the room.

Up on the roof, Robert and Jake were letting themselves into the hangar. They rushed over to the undamaged hoverpod. As Jake tried to jump into the passenger seat, he felt Robert's hand on his shoulder.

"You realise we're going against direct orders here," he said.

"We don't have a choice," replied Jake.

"Don't get me wrong, Jake. I agree," said Robert. "I just wanted to make sure you understand the consequences. We might get kicked out of MI6."

Jake frowned. Robert was right. It was a huge risk, but there wasn't time to think about that. "Sarah's in danger," he said. "Saving her's all that matters."

Robert nodded. The pair jumped into the hoverpod and started the engine.

WHAT HAPPENS NEXT? YOU DECIDE...

Jake drops by

turn to page 42

Sarah gets talking

turn to page 48

jake Drops By

Robert flicked on the camouflage function as the hoverpod blazed out of the hangar. The machine turned midnight blue, blending in perfectly with the night sky as they soared high above the skyscrapers and monuments of London as fast as the hoverpod's engine would allow.

Jake tapped at the hoverpod's onboard computer. Immediately, Sarah's locator beacon appeared and started flashing across the radar screen.

It didn't take them long to home in on the signal and soon they were flying directly above the limo. Robert slowed down to hover above the car.

"What're we gonna do?" asked Jake.

"We need to wait until they're out of London. Somebody's bound to see us if we try anything around here," said Robert as Jake sighed and looked impatient. "Chill out, mate. We'll get her back."

For the next half an hour they watched as the car wound its way out of central London and joined a faster, quieter road heading south.

"Okay, so what's the plan?" said Jake, when they were far enough out of the city.

Robert looked uncomfortable. "Err...I was hoping you'd have one," he said.

Jake sighed and looked down at the speeding car. He had no idea where they were taking Sarah, or what they were planning to do when they got there and he didn't want to hang around to find out. He had to come up with a plan – fast. He closed his eyes and set his brain to work.

Suddenly he clicked his fingers, "I think I've got it!" he cried.

"Excellent! What're you thinking, Jake?" asked Robert, his face lighting up.

Jake didn't answer, he simply called HQ on the hoverpod's radio, "Calling Alex? Come in Alex!" he yelled, urgently.

"Yes, Jake?" came the reply.

"Could we broadcast to the limo's stereo using the hoverpod's radio?" asked Jake, breathlessly.

"I guess so, in theory," said Alex. "You'd need to change the frequency though."

"How do we do that?" said Jake, fidgeting.

"Well, you'd need to change the wiring a little," replied Alex.

"Don't worry, just talk me through it – and make it quick please," said Jake.

Robert kept the hoverpod above the limo as Jake hurriedly re-wired the radio with a screwdriver and a pair of pliers he'd found in a toolbox on the back seat. After ten minutes of prodding and poking, they were almost ready.

"Okay," said Alex. "D'you see the small green switch on the front of the radio?"

"Yeah," said Jake.

"Good. When you flip that switch, keep quiet as everything you say will be broadcast to the limo's radio," warned Alex.

Robert looked at Jake questioningly. "I'm going to try and get a message to Sarah," Jake explained.

"I'd guessed that much, Jake," said Robert indignantly, "But what about whoever's driving the limo? They'll be able to hear it too."

"That's why I'm going to do it in Spanish!" said Jake, producing an auto-translator from his pocket. "Spanish," said Jake clearly into the auto-translator. He took a deep breath, "Let's just hope they've got their radio on."

"And that no one else in that limo speaks Spanish," added Robert, looking worried.

Jake was doing his best to put that possibility out of his mind. "Here goes," he said, flipping the switch.

A few metres below, Sarah was sitting alone in the back of the limo. Her hands were handcuffed and the cold metal was digging into her wrists. She was terrified of what might happen when they got to wherever it was they were going, but she was doing her best to remain calm. There had to be a way out of this.

The radio was playing in the background, but Sarah hadn't noticed until the signal began to crackle and break up. After a while she was vaguely aware of a Spanish voice coming out of the speakers. She looked through the glass window between her and the front of the limo and saw the two men tapping at the radio. For some reason, no matter what they did, the Spanish voice remained.

At first she assumed that it was just interference from a foreign radio station, but as she listened to what the voice was actually saying, she was shocked to hear her own name!

"Sarah? Can you hear me? It's Jake. We're flying above you in the hoverpod."

Sarah smiled. She knew that they would come for her! "Listen carefully," continued the voice in perfect Spanish. "We need you to open the sunroof."

Sarah glanced down at the window controls to her left and subtly pressed the sunroof button. The glass panel slid back and a cold draught filled the car.

Jake breathed a huge sigh of relief as he saw the sunroof slide open beneath them. He high-fived Robert – their message had been received! Jake pulled a pen out of his pocket and wrote a note to Robert. 'GET CLOSER' it read.

Robert nodded and lowered the hoverpod until it was just behind the speeding limo. Fishing in the toolbox again, Jake smiled as he pulled out a length of sturdy rope. He wrapped the rope around his waist and tied it securely, then tied the other end to the head-rest of his seat and tugged it hard to make sure that it would hold.

Jake picked up the auto-translator again. "Sarah, on the count of three, I need you to stand up and put your arms out of the sunroof."

"Good luck, mate" mouthed Robert, who had finally figured out what Jake was planning. Jake nodded nervously as he opened the side door of the hoverpod, "One...two...three!" shouted Jake.

Robert fired the boosters and the hoverpod lurched forwards. Jake launched himself backwards out of the door. The hoverpod swooped over the limo with Jake dangling precariously from it. As he passed over the sunroof, Sarah leapt up. Jake grabbed her arms, dragging her out of the limo and into the air as the hoverpod climbed steeply.

Heron's bodyguards watched, dumbstruck as Sarah sailed into the sky attached, it seemed, to nothing but a boy hanging upside down in thin air.

Sarah looked up at her saviour, the wind blowing and buffeting her as they sped to safety.

"What took you so long?" she grinned.

Now continue to page 59

SaraH GeTS TaLKiNG

Sarah sat alone in the back of Heron's limo, her hands held together by a set of cold, metal handcuffs. Obviously, she was scared but she was also a very sensible girl. Even if she felt like screaming in terror, she knew that it wasn't going to help. If she was going to get out of this, she needed to remain calm and come up with a plan.

Sarah was in the passenger section, separated from her captors by a partition. She could only see the men in the front seats through a narrow glass panel. She couldn't hear their conversation clearly through the panel, especially over the noise of the radio, which was playing pop music. She could see that the two men were deep in conversation.

Sarah wanted to hear what was going on in the front – maybe the men would say something useful. She subtly pressed the intercom button and, as it crackled into life she could faintly hear the sound of a phone ringing. The man in the passenger seat apologised to the driver before picking it up, it was clearly a personal call.

"Da!" said the man in the passenger seat.

Sarah recognised the language immediately; it was Russian! 'Da' was a Russian word for 'yes'. She listened intently to his side of the conversation. He was in trouble with his wife or girlfriend. It seemed she wasn't happy with him working late.

"Oi! Come on," said the driver, in a thick cockney accent. "This ain't no time for domestic strife. We've got a job on!" He seemed angry that his sidekick was distracted. The Russian nodded and, after a few short words, he flicked his mobile shut, silencing the shouting voice at the other end of the phone.

Sarah's brain began to shift into overdrive. She could communicate with one of the guards without the other one understanding. How could she use that to her advantage, though? Suddenly, Sarah felt the car slowing down. "We need petrol," said the driver as he pulled into a service station.

The driver got out of the car and opened the back door. He was an intimidating man with a face like a bulldog and thick, muscly arms. "Don't even think of tryin' any funny business, titch," he warned, as Sarah recoiled. His breath stank of coffee and cigarettes.

Sarah shook her head, "I won't," she replied.

He slammed the door, then sauntered over to the pump. As soon as he was far enough away, Sarah tapped urgently on the glass panel. At first, the Russian man ignored her, but after a while he turned angrily.

"What?" he said, pressing the intercom button.

"I need to talk to you, now," whispered Sarah, in perfect Russian.

The man looked at her, shocked to hear his own language spoken so well by a young English girl.

"About what?" he replied in Russian.

"I have some important information for you," said Sarah, mysteriously.

"Oh yeah, what's that?" scoffed the guard.

Sarah gestured to the driver at the fuel pump. "You mustn't trust him. He's a...spy!" she said, making the story up as she went along.

The Russian responded by laughing heartily. "Frankie's not a spy!"

"Don't talk to her!" the driver shouted from the pump. Although he had noticed the conversation, thankfully he couldn't understand what was actually being said.

Sarah remained deadly serious. "His real name's Dave..." Sarah looked around, trying to think of a surname. The first thing she saw was the newsstand, "Dave...Herald," she continued uncertainly. "He's an undercover cop!"

"And how exactly do you know that?" sneered the Russian man, rolling his eyes.

"I happen to work for the MI6," Sarah said. "And

we know everything."

Despite the fact that this was the first true thing she'd said, it got the biggest laugh from the Russian guard. "You? You're only a child!" he said, his face twisting with cruel laughter.

"Oi!" yelled Frankie, from across the forecourt. "Last chance, fella. Shut it," he threatened.

Sarah had to think fast, "I may look like a child," she said, "but that's only because I have a rare disease that stops me growing..." she continued, getting carried away with her elaborate lie, "I'm actually twenty-five. It's the perfect cover! No one suspects I'm a spy! Do you think I'd be able to speak perfect Russian if I was just a kid?"

The Russian guard's brow furrowed slightly. He clearly wasn't the sharpest knife in the drawer, and Sarah could tell that he was starting to believe her, or at least to entertain the possibility that she might be telling the truth.

"Look!" she said in Russian, urgently. "I know for a fact he met with the police last night!" Sarah saw Frankie striding angrily towards the limo. She had to work quickly! "Ask him what he was doing last night. You're obviously a smart guy. You can tell when someone's lying, can't you?" said Sarah, frantically.

The Russian beamed at Sarah's compliment. Just then, Frankie yanked open the door. "You stupid or what? What's going on here?" he shouted.

"A...a...ask him!" stuttered Sarah.

"Shut up, titch!" yelled Frankie, as he turned to the Russian and scowled. "I thought I told you not to talk to her!"

The Russian looked at Sarah and she nodded solemnly at him. He turned to the driver, "Frankie, I need a word – in private," he said.

"What?" said the driver.

The Russian took him by the arm and led him to the edge of the petrol station.

This was Sarah's chance, but she had to move quickly. Her captors may have been dumb, but even they would realise she was lying soon enough. She tested the electronic windows but, as she had suspected, they were locked. Luckily, they had forgotten to do the same with the sunroof. She

grinned as she watched the glass panel slide back.

Sarah looked out of the window. The two men were involved in a furious argument. Probably because the Russian had just accused Frankie of being an undercover cop – something you don't say to a criminal! She waited until both were looking away and then sprang into action. She slid out of the sunroof and dropped quietly on to the concrete.

Sarah thought about running away, but decided it wasn't an option, with them in a car and her on foot, they'd soon catch up with her.

She crept around to the side of the car and let herself in through the passenger side door. She was going to have to 'borrow' Heron's limo. The driver had taken the car keys with him, but luckily, a while ago Alex had shown her how to start a vehicle without keys. She just hoped she could remember how to do it. It was called 'hot-wiring'. It was difficult with newer cars, but older models like this limo were fairly easy.

Sarah started to remove the protective panel underneath the steering wheel. She was still wearing the handcuffs so it was pretty tough going, but eventually it fell to the floor, revealing the wires that led from the ignition to the engine. She thought for a moment and then ripped two out and stripped away the plastic insulation with her nails. Sarah held her breath as she touched the exposed wires together and the engine stuttered into life.

Quick as a flash, she sat up in the driver's seat, stamped on the accelerator and the car lurched into motion. She swung the steering wheel around with her cuffed hands as, out of the corner of her eye, she saw the men running back towards the car. She jolted up and down in the seat as the limo bumped up over a concrete kerb and back on to the motorway, narrowly avoiding the oncoming cars.

"You muppet! She's escaping," yelled Frankie to the Russian. He thought for a moment before pulling out a gun and running over to a woman who was filling up her car. "Out of the way!" he shouted at her, waving the weapon.

She screamed as the two men pushed past and jumped into her car. Within seconds they'd screeched out of the service station in hot pursuit of the limo.

Limos, in fact, cars in general, tend not to be designed for twelve year-olds to drive, especially not twelve year-olds in handcuffs. Sarah was not only having trouble seeing over the dashboard and reaching the pedals, she also had to take her hands off the steering wheel every time she needed to change gear. All of which was making this particular car chase very dangerous indeed as she weaved across the road at high speed. She craned her neck, managing to look in the rear view mirror as she dodged through the traffic. Suddenly, Sarah saw a small car approaching. That must be them, she thought frantically, as they steadily gained on her.

Fortunately for Sarah, Heron's guards weren't the only people following her. Robert and Jake had been flying above the limo in the hoverpod trying to find an opportunity to save her. They had watched with delight as she stole the limo and were now determined to help her complete her daring escape.

"We need to slow them down!" said Jake, urgently.

"Hang on, I've got an idea!" replied Robert.

He lowered the hoverpod closer to the chasing car. He could see the passenger window was half open.

"Any good at cricket, Jake?" asked Robert.

"I'm okay…" responded Jake, surprised to be asked that question when Sarah was in danger. "Why?"

"Do you think you could throw this through that window?" replied Robert, producing a small grey ball with what looked like a piece of string poking out of the top.

"Maybe, what is it?"

"It's a smoke bomb. I sometimes use them in my shows," he said, handing it to Jake, along with a book of matches from his pocket. "Light the wick and throw it," he added.

Jake struck a match and ignited the end of the string. The wick began burning slowly.

Robert looked back to the road. "Wait!" he yelled suddenly. They were rapidly approaching a bridge. Robert pulled back heavily on the joystick, just managing to avoid it. As Robert manoeuvred the hoverpod back into position, Jake noticed with horror that the wick had almost burned down. Throwing it quickly at the small car, Jake breathed a huge sigh of relief as it bounced off the edge of the window and dropped inside, sending plumes of smoke billowing around the interior.

Before they knew what had happened, the guards' car was filled with thick, grey smoke. Soon, they couldn't see a thing. They skidded and swerved, finally ploughing the car into the barrier in the centre of the motorway as other cars swerved out of the way and skidded to a halt behind them.

Sarah looked into the limo's rear view mirror and grinned triumphantly as she noticed the chasing car slowly disappearing into the distance behind her. She didn't know what had happened, but she was certainly relieved. But then reality began to dawn. She couldn't keep driving in handcuffs, it wasn't safe. Plus, if she got pulled over by the police which, considering her driving, seemed a distinct possibility, they might have a few questions to ask about what a twelve year-old was doing driving a limo – and a stolen one at that. That was a hassle she didn't need.

She was going to have to pull over and wait for the kids to follow her distress beacon and find her. Sarah turned on her left indicator and pulled the limo over on to the hard shoulder. She opened the passenger side door, slid out and hauled herself over the barrier and up on to the grass verge.

Sarah sat down and sighed as she looked down at her outfit, which was crumpled and torn. She thought about everything that had happened that night. It seemed like days since she had walked into the fancy London party, yet only a few hours had passed. More to the point, Sarah wondered how on earth she was going to save the Prime Minister from whatever fate Heron had planned.

Suddenly, a rope ladder flopped down in front of her. Sarah looked up. At first glance, the ladder appeared to be floating in the night sky, but soon her eyes adjusted. It was the hoverpod! Jake climbed down the ladder to her.

"Hey, Sarah," he said. "Need a lift?"

Sarah grinned from ear to ear. "You took your time!" she replied teasingly, as Jake helped her on to the ladder.

Once she was safely seated in the back seat of the hoverpod, Sarah hugged Robert and Jake enthusiastically. The engines kicked in, and they sped back to base.

4
THE SWITCH

It was close to midnight. Inside 10 Downing Street, Jonathan Holmes was sitting at his vast oak desk. He looked at the clock and sighed. It was no use trying to work, he couldn't concentrate. His argument with Heron was weighing heavily on his mind.

Most of the government had been taken in by Heron's slick presentation and smooth patter earlier that evening, but Jonathan was now certain that Heron could not be trusted. Telling his fellow MPs at tomorrow's cabinet meeting was going to be tricky, to say the least. Jonathan yawned. He was waiting for Sarah Moore to arrive. She had called to schedule an urgent meeting, saying it couldn't wait until morning. Jonathan hoped she might have some evidence to back up his suspicions about Heron.

He began to pace absent-mindedly. Now that he came to think about it, Sarah had sounded really odd on the phone. She was usually so calm and level-headed, but tonight he had detected a note of panic in her voice. And why was she so insistent that he shouldn't see anyone else before she arrived?

Jonathan's phone buzzed, breaking his thoughts. He wandered back to the desk and picked it up.

"Mr Heron just called, Sir," said Jonathan's personal assistant, Sue. "He's on his way home from the party and wondered if he might pop in to see you for a moment. He said it couldn't wait," she added.

That was a surprise, thought Jonathan. Heron was the last person he was expecting to see, especially at this time of night. Jonathan thought he had made his feelings clear, but it seemed Heron wasn't going to give up easily. Whatever it was, Jonathan was too tired to deal with him. "Tell him it's too late, Sue," he sighed.

"Will do. He said something about wanting to apologise," said Sue.

The Prime Minister usually liked to believe the best of people. Over the years he'd found that it was better to try to get along with people, even those he disagreed with. Perhaps he should give Heron the chance to apologise. It would only take five minutes and he had to wait up for Sarah anyway. It might stop Heron from pestering him until he'd had the chance to persuade the cabinet to back Sir Brian's plans...

"Okay, he can have five minutes, Sue," said Jonathan sighing. "Then go home. It's very late."

60

Soon there was a sharp knock at the door and Heron stepped smartly into the room. He was smiling, but looked slightly sheepish. "Prime Minister," he said apologetically. "Thank you so much for seeing me at this late hour."

"Rufus," said Jonathan, doing his best to smile as he shook his hand.

"I just wanted to see you to clear up our little misunderstanding earlier..."

"Misunderstanding?" repeated Jonathan, trying to disguise his disbelief.

"Yes, Prime Minister. I was aghast that you thought I was offering you some kind of bribe. I pride myself on being a thoroughly open and honest businessman, so in the spirit of this, I have come to apologise and to ask you for a second chance. If you outline your concerns, my team and I will work through the night to make the proposal succeed."

Jonathan smiled; he had never seen this side of Heron before. "Well, Rufus, I'm glad to hear you say that," he replied warmly. "First and foremost, you need to start thinking about the environmental..."

He was interrupted by a loud knock at the door. "Come in," said Jonathan, thinking it might be Sarah.

The door opened and a young woman pushed a tea trolley through the door. That's strange, thought Jonathan, he didn't recognise her at all.

"I took the liberty of asking your assistant to

arrange tea for us, Prime Minister," said Heron, smoothly. "I hope you don't mind."

"Not at all," replied Jonathan, eyeing the tea lady suspiciously. Gladys usually served tea in the evenings.

"Something wrong, Prime Minister?" asked Rufus.

"No, nothing," Jonathan replied. I'm just being paranoid, he thought. Gladys was probably off sick. "I'd love some tea, thank you."

The woman smiled and poured the tea. Jonathan leaned informally against the side of his desk and took a sip. Heron placed his cup on the desk. "I'll let mine cool," he said.

"Rufus, the major problem with your city plans is that..." Jonathan tailed off. For some reason he'd lost his train of thought. "Sorry," he said, taking another sip of tea to collect himself. "The thing is..." Out of nowhere, Jonathan had suddenly become incredibly tired. He didn't know what had come over him.

"Prime Minister, are you okay?" smirked Heron.

"I'm a little sshleepy tha's..." Jonathan couldn't continue. He stumbled, struggling to keep his footing. As he looked down at the cup of tea, then up at Heron's impassive face, a chill ran down his spine. The tea was drugged! That was why he didn't recognise the tea lady, she must be working for Heron. How could he have been so foolish? Jonathan struggled to focus on Heron as his eyes became heavy. "You'll never get away with..." His words faded to a mumble as he fell forwards with a heavy crash.

"Such a shame, Jonathan," said Heron, nudging the Prime Minister's motionless body with his foot. "I liked you. We could have been a great team. As I said, we're going to work through the night to make sure the proposal succeeds..."

He looked at the woman behind the tea trolley and nodded. She lifted the top off the trolley and out popped Henry. He was wearing different clothes now, and a wig to cover his baldness. Heron smiled at Henry. Plan B was coming together nicely.

Henry Allinson was an actor, a good one too – he had been well-known in the nineties. But as well as his acting skills, there was a particular thing that made him the perfect man for the job – he looked almost identical to the Prime Minister. Dressed as he was in the wig and the right clothes, it was almost impossible to tell the difference.

Several months ago Heron's assistant, Snidley, had approached Henry with an acting job. They had offered him a lot of money to play the Prime Minister. Not on stage, not in a film, but for real.

Henry said yes almost immediately. He was a very selfish man who desperately needed the money, even if it involved breaking the law on a massive scale. Henry had spent the last two months preparing to be the Prime Minister. He had learnt his life story, studied videos of him and practised his movements and voice. Now his impression was so spot on that even Jonathan's own mother would struggle to tell them apart.

Henry climbed out of the tea trolley, as Heron eyed him critically. He would never tell him so, but Snidley had done a good job finding this man. Henry looked identical to Jonathan Holmes in every way, from his mannerisms, right down to his hair and clothes.

"Ready?" he asked, sternly.

"Absolutely," replied Henry. His impersonation of the Prime Minister really was perfect.

"Feeling confident?" asked Heron, his eyes narrowing accusingly.

"Of course," said Henry.

"Keep it simple," warned Heron. "You know what the consequences will be if this goes wrong..."

Henry gave an involuntary shudder. Heron could be so chilling sometimes.

Heron leaned casually against the desk as the tea lady and Henry bundled Jonathan into the tea trolley. They replaced the lid and the woman wheeled him out of the office without a word.

"Who's she and what's she going to do with him?" asked Henry.

"You don't need to know," snapped Heron.

"He...he's still alive, isn't he?" stuttered Henry. He was starting to feel nervous.

"I suggest you focus your attention on the performance ahead," said Heron, calmly. "Good luck," he added, before picking up his coat to leave.

Henry winced. "Never say good luck to an actor, old boy! It's terribly unlucky," he said. "We say 'break a leg'."

Heron raised an eyebrow. "If you don't pull this off, you'll have more than a broken leg," he said darkly, before turning and walking out of the office.

Henry was left alone to contemplate the enormous challenge ahead. He was about to embark on the biggest job of his life. His months of work and research had all been building up to this moment. Henry smiled nervously as he imagined himself stepping on to the stage as the curtain went up.

5
suspicious Behaviour

Sarah flinched as the hoverpod slowed down to land on the roof of MI6. Jake had found a pair of bolt-cutters in the tool box and removed one of the handcuffs. He was just about through with the other and when the hoverpod landed, it finally snapped open. Sarah jumped out before Robert had turned off the engine. Jake and Robert rushed to catch up with her as she sprinted out of the hangar, down the stairs, into the depths of the M.I.Five HQ.

Sarah hadn't forgotten what she'd heard in the car park. Heron was planning something big and it sounded as if the Prime Minister was in danger. She wasn't going to sit back and let that happen. Sarah had already called Jonathan from the hoverpod to schedule an urgent meeting. She'd asked him to wait in his office and, most importantly, not to see anyone until she arrived. She would explain the rest face-to-face. He'd been reluctant at first, especially as it was so late, but he respected Sarah's opinion and could tell that she was worried, so in the end he'd agreed.

Sarah strode down the hallway in her filthy, tattered outfit, completely focused on two things. The first was to check that the Prime Minister was safe, then she'd make sure that the slimy Heron was sorted out once and for all.

"Nobody kidnaps Sarah Moore and gets away with it," she said to herself, crossly.

"Who is this Heron bloke?" Robert asked Jake as they raced down the hallway after Sarah.

"Not sure," replied Jake, "But he's messed with the wrong girl!"

Sarah dashed into the crisis room and grabbed the phone. "I need a car!" she said, urgently. "Where to...? Downing Street...yes I do know what time it is...please, just get it here ASAP – this is an emergency!" she cried.

"Sarah, cancel that car," ordered Julian from the doorway. As soon as Jake and Robert had left MI6 to find Sarah, Julian had set off for HQ. He had to take charge and deal with this defiance. Julian always looked stern, but none of the kids had ever seen him like this. He was livid! Chun Mai and Alex followed him into the room. They both looked upset – Julian had read them the riot act. Chun Mai's eyes were red as if she had been crying, but the moment they saw Sarah, his angry words were forgotten.

"Sarah!" shouted Chun Mai. "I'm so glad you're safe!" she said, as she and Alex rushed over to give her a hug.

Even Julian's face softened a little. "Good to have you back, Sarah," he said. "But the fact remains," he said, his stern look returning, "that what you did was dangerous and directly against orders." As he paused to let his words sink in, the kids shifted uncomfortably. "I have never, in all my time here, come across such disobedience. You are lucky you weren't killed. As agents you must respect and obey the rules. If you can't, we'll have to reassess whether you are suited to working for MI6."

Jake gulped and looked at his friends. The kids knew from Julian's eyebrows that they were in trouble and they all looked suitably shamefaced. "Now I'm here, I want a complete debrief from you, immediately."

"It will have to wait, Agent Morris," said Sarah. "We're off to Downing Street to see Jonathan Holmes."

"Out of the question," said Julian. "Whatever it is, it can wait…"

"You don't understand, Julian," interrupted Sarah. "This can't wait. I left a message on his mobile earlier. He's waiting for me now."

"You have the Prime Minister's mobile number?" said Julian, incredulously.

"Yeah, he gave it to me a couple of months ago," replied Sarah, casually.

Julian gathered his thoughts. He was still furious that the kids had disobeyed him but, secretly, he was also a little impressed. Julian knew a lot of people – decision makers and other VIPs. But he was sure that only a handful of them would have the Prime Minister's mobile number.

"Very well," he said finally. "But I'll come too. Brief me on the way."

"Thanks, Julian," said Sarah, rushing past him. The rest of the kids followed, all apart from Jake, who found his path blocked by Julian, whose eyebrows were moving rapidly with frustration.

"As the leader of the little rebellion today, a number of people wanted you out of MI6. You were stupid and reckless," he began. "Let me make myself clear: if you step out of line again, it will be out of my hands..."

Jake nodded, guiltily. He understood what Julian was saying. It was time to play by the rules.

"I'm serious. Don't throw away your future, Jake," warned Julian.

"I won't let you down, Agent Morris," promised Jake. He was going to have to be careful not to break the rules again.

Sarah twiddled her thumbs nervously as the car made the short journey to Downing Street through the nighttime streets. What if she was too late? What if Jonathan didn't believe her? Come to think of it, what was she going to say? She didn't know much, just that

Heron was planning something, and it was unlikely to be a surprise party! Before she knew it, the car was at the gates. Julian flashed his security card at a guard on the gate. The guard looked into the back of the car and nodded at Sarah; by now he was used to seeing her coming and going.

When they got to the Prime Minister's office, Sue was about to go home. "Hi, Sarah," she said as she put her coat on. "You can go straight through, he's expecting you."

"Has he had any visitors since my call, Sue?" asked Sarah, breathlessly.

Sue was a little taken aback by Sarah's urgency, she was usually such a calm girl. "Err, no, I don't think so." Sarah breathed a huge sigh of relief. "Oh, actually, I tell a lie," said Sue. "He did have a brief meeting with Rufus Heron."

"Heron!" gasped Sarah in horror as she rushed into the office.

"She's so strange," muttered Sue as she grabbed her bag and headed for the door.

Rushing into the office, Sarah breathed a deep sigh of relief as she saw the Prime Minister looking at one of the pictures on the wall. Little did she know that she was too late – Jonathan had been wheeled out in the tea trolley moments earlier.

"Prime Minister!" exclaimed Sarah. "Am I glad to see you!"

As Henry turned around, he struggled to hide his surprise. A man and five children had come in. What's more, one of them was the girl from the car park. Henry thought she'd been dealt with by Heron's bodyguards. How was he going to bluff his way through this one?

Henry composed himself. "Where else would I

be?" he said. "I am the Prime Minister," he added somewhat unnecessarily.

"Err...yeah, we know," muttered Chun Mai under her breath. Julian shot her an icy look and she shut up immediately.

"I'm afraid Agent Moore was abducted earlier, Prime Minister," said Julian, gravely.

"Goodness!" said Henry. "Is she okay?"

"Yes, thank you," replied Sarah. "But no thanks to Rufus Heron," she added, fiercely.

Henry started. She was Agent Moore? That couldn't be right – she was just a child! "Rufus Heron?" asked Henry, pretending to know nothing about it. "What on earth did he have to do with it?"

"He's the one who kidnapped me!" said Sarah, impatiently. "To stop me warning you that he's up to no good...and whatever it is, it involves you."

Henry started to panic. This little brat was on to them. Luckily she didn't appear to know any details and she'd been taken in completely by his disguise. He had to do something – fast!

"That's utterly ridiculous," he said. "Why would an honest, decent businessman like Mr Heron kidnap anyone? As for hurting me, that's preposterous. In fact, he's just left. We had a very productive meeting."

"But, Sir," said Sarah, "I'm telling the truth. Heron had me kidnapped!"

Henry looked over at Julian and shrugged. "I think

someone's got an overactive imagination," he said.

Sarah's face flushed with embarrassment and rage. She hated being treated like some silly little child. "You're wrong!" snapped Sarah, furiously.

"Agent Moore! Show some respect, please!" warned Julian.

Henry looked at her sternly. "It appears you've forgotten your manners, young lady. I am the Prime Minister, after all."

"So you keep saying," said Chun Mai, muttering to herself.

"I'm so sorry we've wasted your time, Prime Minister," said Julian.

"If I were you, I'd focus my attention on finding out who abducted your agent, rather than throwing around these outrageous accusations," snapped Henry. "Now if you'll excuse me, I'm going to bed. And I suggest you do the same, children. It's way past your bedtime."

"But Jonathan, what are you saying?" said Sarah, shocked. "You told me you'd never trust Heron, but now you're...defending him?"

"That's right," replied Henry, coolly. "I misjudged him. After our meeting just now, he's convinced me that he's the right man to build these Future Cities."

Sarah stood open-mouthed. She couldn't believe what she was hearing. But as Julian began shepherding the kids out of the office, she had a thought. She turned to the Prime Minister and started to speak in fluent French. "Don't you believe me? Why not? It's the truth, I swear!"

As Henry stared at her in complete confusion, Sarah looked back at him with a strange look on her face. However, her reasoning behind this sudden switch into French was lost on everyone else. Had the stress of the evening been too much for her? Had she had some sort of breakdown?

Julian was baffled and embarrassed in equal measure. "Time to go, Agent Moore," he said, grabbing Sarah's shoulder firmly and steering her away. But as she was pushed out of the door she raised her voice and close to shouted in French, "Are you the real Prime Minister?"

"What's she babbling on about?" laughed Henry.

Julian practically dragged Sarah out of the office and stalked out of Downing Street as the kids hurried to keep up. In the car, nobody spoke. The kids were far too shocked and Julian looked as if he was about to explode with rage. Sarah was deep in thought. Something had occurred to her back there. It was so far-fetched that it was almost unbelievable. Could she really trust her instincts on this one?

6

a CHange of HearT

Up on the roof of M.I.Five HQ, Sarah was looking out across the city. She'd just come out of a meeting with Julian. He had ranted at her for disobeying orders and for making a fool of him in front of the Prime Minister. Sarah's ears were still ringing from his angry words. But worst of all, he'd made her take the day off.

Sarah was annoyed that she'd been banned from working but there wasn't much she could have done, even if she was allowed to. Julian had ordered the kids to close their investigation into Heron. Sarah didn't doubt herself for a minute, she knew what she had heard in the car park – Heron was planning something big, but what? Sarah needed to clear her head. She decided to go for a walk.

Wrapping herself up in a heavy overcoat, Sarah wandered along the banks of the River Thames. What was Heron up to? If he wanted to hurt the Prime

Minister, he'd had the perfect opportunity during their meeting last night, but it seemed that all he'd done was have a friendly chat and leave. Unless...

Deep in thought, Sarah passed a woman pushing a double buggy. Two little boys, dressed in identical clothing, gazed up at her as she walked by. And with that, the niggling thought she'd first had last night popped back into her head. She'd been thinking about it up on the roof, too, but in the cold light of day it had seemed so ridiculous, so far-fetched that she'd dismissed it. But Sarah had to face it – this stubborn little notion wouldn't go away. The shout of a newspaper seller interrupted her thoughts.

"Decision on Future Cities announced. Read all about it...," called the seller.

What? thought Sarah, frantically, as she fished some coins from her purse and bought a paper. Scanning the article, she discovered that it was true, the government had made the decision on the Future Cities. Sarah's eyes widened as she looked at the photo of the Prime Minister shaking hands with Rufus Heron. According to the paper, the deal had been announced by the Prime Minister earlier that morning. It was worth billions and he'd awarded it to Heron, even though he'd told Sarah less than twenty-four hours earlier that he didn't trust him. It just didn't make sense!

Sarah sprinted away from the news stand. She had to get back to HQ. The moment she'd seen that photo in the paper, any doubts that she'd had disappeared. It was the only explanation. The man she'd met with last night at 10 Downing Street was not the real Jonathan Holmes; he was an impostor!

When Sarah got back, the first person she saw was Jake. He was sitting in the living room staring in confusion at the evening news. The TV screen was showing footage of a joint press conference between Heron and the Prime Minister.

"So you've heard then?" said Sarah, taking in Jake's shocked expression.

Jake nodded. Sarah watched Heron; he was

smiling smugly while the Prime Minister gave a speech about Heron's new cities.

"Our future is in the hands of Mr Heron and he will change the face of Britain for ever..." proclaimed the Prime Minister.

Sarah felt sick. As the Prime Minister continued to speak, she became ever more certain she was right. She noticed little hand gestures and verbal ticks that seemed out of place. There was no way that man was Jonathan Holmes. The man on TV was doing a very convincing impersonation of the Prime Minister, but it wasn't perfect. Too right Britain would be changing. It would be a nightmare, she thought, gloomily.

"Sarah," said Jake. "I don't get it. I thought you said the Prime Minister hated Heron?"

"We need to get everyone together," replied Sarah solemnly. "There's something I need to explain."

"Okay," said Jake, a little confused.

As soon as everyone had gathered in Sarah's room, Robert spoke. "What's up?" he asked. "Why aren't we meeting in the crisis room?"

"Julian mustn't know about this meeting," warned Sarah. "He'll never believe what I'm about to say, plus if he hears me mention Heron's name he'll go nuclear."

"Can you just tell us what's going on, Sarah," demanded Alex.

Sarah took a deep breath. "Remember yesterday

in the Prime Minister's office, when I started shouting in French?"

"Yeah," said Chun Mai. "What was that about? I thought you'd lost the plot."

"Yeah, well, it must have seemed odd if you didn't know why," admitted Sarah. "It was a test. You see, the Prime Minister speaks perfect French. He's even better than me," she continued. "But when I spoke it to him last night he didn't understand a word..."

"And?" said Chun Mai, baffled.

"People don't just forget a language, Chun Mai," said Sarah. "So it means only one thing. The man we met with last night is not the real Prime Minister!"

The kids goggled at her. They weren't sure what to say. Sarah had expected this reaction. She wasn't sure she'd have believed it herself if someone had said it to her. It all sounded so dramatic.

"Look, it's the only possible explanation," she said. "Jonathan can't stand Heron. He said last night that he prefers Sir Brian's plan. Do you think he'd switch sides overnight? There must be something fishy going on." The kids nodded thoughtfully, though clearly they were having trouble processing the information.

"I don't know," said Robert. "Politicians change their minds all the time."

"Not Jonathan Holmes. He was dead set against Heron's plan last night. I don't think a five minute meeting would make him change his mind," said

Sarah, desperate for her friends to believe her.

"It does seem a bit weird..." admitted Chun Mai. "And did you guys notice how he kept saying last night, 'I am the Prime Minister'? It all seemed a bit...well... fake," she added, slowly.

"Is Heron really so evil?" asked Alex. "I mean, kidnapping the Prime Minister just to make a shed-load of money?"

"Money makes people do crazy stuff, Alex," said Jake. "You know what, Sarah, I think you could be right," he added.

"I believe you, too," said Chun Mai.

"If you really think about it, well, it's mad, but it does make sense. More sense than Jonathan changing his mind overnight, anyway," added Alex.

The kids all looked towards Robert, "I think it's crazy," he said. Sarah frowned; she was a little hurt. "But then again," he added, "crazy things happen. I mean, look at Jean-Paul Laurent. That seemed pretty mad, too. Are you one hundred per cent sure?"

"Absolutely," replied Sarah, firmly.

"Then I am too," said Robert.

Sarah grinned; she was glad her friends were behind her.

"How did Heron and his cronies manage it d'you think?" asked Jake.

"Heron must have made the switch at some point during the meeting last night," said Sarah. "If only Julian hadn't held us up..." she said, thumping her desk in frustration.

"So, if it's not the Prime Minister in Downing Street, who is it?" wondered Chun Mai. "And what have they done with the real one?"

"I don't know," said Sarah, "But we have to find out! You can't just kidnap the Prime Minister because he makes a decision you don't like!"

"Not while the M.I.Five are around, anyway," added Chun Mai, angrily.

7

roBerT's Big iDea

Several hours later, Sarah, Robert, Alex and Jake were still in Sarah's room. They reasoned that Julian was so annoyed with Sarah that it would be the last place he'd go. Even so, they had set up a game of chess so that if he did walk in on them, he wouldn't suspect anything was going on. In reality, they were engaged in a top secret conspiracy.

Right now, however, it wasn't much of a conspiracy. They didn't even have a plan. Coming up with one was really hard – they weren't even sure where to begin. They knew next to nothing about Heron and even less about where he might be holding Jonathan Holmes. Their task wasn't made any easier by the fact that they had to avoid Julian, too. If he found out that they were investigating Heron, they'd all be in serious trouble. Jake had told them what Julian had said to him the night before. By going against his orders again, they were in danger of being kicked out of MI6.

Without a single lead, they were getting nowhere fast. The kids sighed, almost in unison. They had nothing to go on.

"Sarah, I've been thinking," began Jake, quietly. "The thing is, how do we...err...how do we know that Jonathan's still, you know...?"

"Alive?" interrupted Sarah.

"Yeah," said Jake, awkwardly.

"Well, we don't really know for sure," she replied solemnly. "We just have to hope that Heron is holding him somewhere until the deal goes through."

Just then, Chun Mai arrived at the door. She was stony-faced and clutching a laptop. Chun Mai had sneaked off to her computer room a while ago to look into Heron Construction and maybe hack into their system. The kids had assumed that even if Julian did walk in, he wouldn't understand what she was doing anyway – nobody ever did.

"Find anything useful, Chun Mai?" asked Sarah, glad for the distraction.

"No, it was a complete waste of time," said Chun Mai, crossly. "I hacked into the Heron system in, like, five minutes, it was embarrassingly easy. There was only one file that was really protected. It took me ages to open it."

"What was in there?" asked Jake, hopefully.

"That's the annoying thing! When I eventually got

in, all I found was this," she said, placing her laptop on top of the chess board, so that everyone could see. On the screen was a list of materials and quantities with prices next to them.

"What's that?" asked Robert, staring at the seemingly meaningless list of numbers.

"It's a budget," said Jake, looking intently at the screen. "It shows all the materials they'll need to build the cities, how much of everything they'll need and what it'll cost."

"Pretty useless, huh?" said Chun Mai, shrugging.

"Nice try, Chun Mai. Never mind, we'll just have to..." Sarah began.

"Hang on a minute!" said Alex interrupting her as he flicked through the budget. "Why on earth are they planning to use untreated carbon steel?" he asked, as the rest of the kids looked back at Alex blankly.

"You're going to need to translate that into English for us, Alex," said Jake.

"It's one of the cheapest kinds of steel you can buy. There's no way it's strong enough to support the kinds of skyscrapers and stadiums they want to build. I can't believe they'd be so idiotic. The buildings will be dangerous!" he cried.

Alex kept flicking through the pages of the budget, gasping every now and then as he discovered another dangerous cost-cutting measure. Pretty soon it was clear that everything in Heron's cities, from the glass and bricks to the concrete, was going to be made of the cheapest materials, whether or not they were safe.

"Heron's Future Cities will be death-traps!" said Alex, in alarm.

"Blimey," said Chun Mai. "How tight can you get?"

"'Bigger, better cities...for half the price.' That's what Heron said," said Sarah, thinking back to his glossy presentation. "And now we know how he's going to do it."

"This is a nightmare," said Alex. "We can't let him build these cities!"

"Let's show Heron Construction's budget plans to the government." said Robert.

"We can't," said Jake.

"Jake's right. This isn't proof," explained Sarah. "Heron could just say they were old plans...or for something else."

"Plus, we'd have to explain how we got hold of it," added Chun Mai. "It's a stolen document, remember. We'll get kicked out of MI6 if Julian finds out!"

"Okay. So we can't tell Julian and we can't tell the government. Who's the one person who could stop those cities being built?" asked Jake. "We need to find the Prime Minister. If we can prove that Heron kidnapped him, the deal would be over in a flash!"

"But how are we supposed to find the Prime Minister?" said Robert, frustrated. "I mean, some of us don't even know who this Heron guy is. I couldn't even tell you what he looked like," he added.

"You really should watch the news every now and then, Robert," said Sarah briskly, shaking her head at Robert's ignorance.

Chun Mai tapped a few keys on her laptop and turned the screen to face Robert. "There you go," she said, showing Robert a picture from a news website. It was of Heron shaking hands with the fake Prime Minister. "Happy now?" she asked.

Robert stared hard at the screen, a glimmer of recognition passing his face. "That's Heron?" he said, grinning broadly.

"Yeah," said Sarah. "Do you know him?"

"Not personally, I'm pleased to say," said Robert. "But he always sponsors a big magic convention every year. Apparently, he loves illusions."

The kids laughed. Heron liked magic? It didn't seem likely.

"No, seriously, he does!" Robert insisted.

"He's right!" said Chun Mai.

She had just typed 'Heron' and 'magic' into a search engine and found hundreds of articles. She clicked on one that read 'Heron shells out for third magic convention.' It revealed a huge picture of Heron clapping a magician on the back, at a glitzy casino.

"Actually," said Robert, "According to some of the magicians I know, he's a bit of a pain. He always wants to know how our illusions are done. He even offered the Great Mysterio money if he'd share his secrets. The Great Mysterio was really upset about it."

"Did he tell Heron his secrets?" asked Chun Mai.

"No, he refused," said Robert. "But soon after, he disappeared from the magic scene. No one knows what happened to him," he added.

Sarah gasped. "You don't think...?"

"Who knows," shrugged Robert.

"Hang on, Rob. If Heron's so famous amongst magicians, how come you didn't recognise his name?" asked Jake.

"I've only ever heard him referred to by his nickname," said Robert.

"What's that?" asked Jake.

"He's known as the Hawk!" replied Robert darkly, flapping his arms by his sides. "Because he hovers around magicians, waiting to strike."

"This is all very interesting, guys," said Sarah. "But it's not getting us any closer to finding Jonathan!"

"Maybe we could steal Heron's phone?" suggested Jake. "Or his computer?"

"So, how're we going to steal anything from a man who has body guards and assistants?" asked Chun Mai. Jake shrugged his shoulders. "It's not as if he's just going to hand them over."

"Maybe we could look for clues at his office?" said Alex, hopefully.

"You can't just walk into a company that size,"

replied Sarah. "His head office will be absolutely crawling with security."

The kids slumped around the room frowning dejectedly, all except for Robert. He had a broad smile on his face, the beginnings of an idea were forming in his mind. "Guys," he said, finally, "I know how we can get into his office."

"How?" asked Sarah, eagerly.

"Magic! That's how! I'm going to turn up at Heron's office tomorrow and put on a surprise show for him," he said, grinning from ear to ear as the others smiled uneasily. "'The Hawk' won't be able to resist a private show from one of the best magicians in the world!" added Robert, smugly.

"Or you, if he's unavailable," joked Chun Mai.

"Whatever, computer geek," Robert shot back.

"You know, that's not a bad idea, Robert," said Jake, impressed.

"Of course, I'll need a glamorous assistant to help me," said Robert. "Are you up for it, Sarah? I'm sure you've got a glitzy outfit in your wardrobe," he added with a grin.

"You know I'd do it if I could," said Sarah. "But Heron has already seen me. I can't go strolling into his office after he kidnapped me and I trashed his limo, can I?"

"You're right," said Robert. He turned to Chun Mai, grinning as he spotted his chance to get his own back for her sarcastic digs.

"Don't look at me!" begged Chun Mai. "I'm not doing it! You know I don't do dresses." She was panicking. As a lifelong tomboy, the idea of putting on a sparkly dress and prancing about with Robert filled her with horror. "Why does it have to be me? Why can't one of the boys be your assistant?" she said, in increasing desperation.

"Sorry, Chun Mai, magician's assistants are usually girls," said Jake, trying not to laugh. "We have to make this look realistic, otherwise Heron'll get suspicious."

"I don't care!" cried Chun Mai, defiantly. "Even if the Prime Minister is in danger, I'm not doing it. I won't wear a dress!" The rest of the kids continued looking at her pleadingly. "Come on, guys, you know how I feel about dresses. I'll look like a dork," she muttered.

8
THE SHOW

Chun Mai pulled a face as she struggled down the street towards Heron Construction's offices. She was tired after staying up late to learn Robert's stupid magic routine and, to cap it all, she looked completely ridiculous. The sequined dress she'd borrowed from Sarah was really scratchy and she was struggling to walk in a pair of strappy shoes that hurt her feet. She wished that she was wrapped up in her beloved hoodie and comfy trainers.

"Come on, Chun Mai," said Robert, pacing ahead in his top hat and tails.

Chun Mai muttered something under her breath as she struggled with the crate of magic equipment she was wheeling behind her.

"You know, you could help me with some of this..." grumbled Chun Mai.

"I'm sorry, but The Great Roberto doesn't carry his

own equipment," grinned Robert. "That wouldn't look right at all."

Bumping the crate up the steps, Chun Mai wedged herself and the magic gear into the revolving doors. "Careful, Chun Mai! Some of that equipment is very valuable, you know," said Robert.

"Can I help you?" asked the baffled security guard when they approached the desk.

"We're here to perform for Mr Rufus Heron," said Robert grandly. "It's a surprise. He's a great fan of mine," he added.

"Well, there's nothing about it on my visitors' list," said the security guard, tapping the clipboard that he kept behind his desk. "And if your name's not down, you're not coming in," he added, making the most of his chance to use his favourite catchphrase.

Robert sighed heavily. "My good man," he said, as if he were explaining something very complicated to a small child. "The show is supposed to be a surprise for Mr Heron. It wouldn't be much of a surprise if everyone knew, now would it?"

The security guard frowned and cleared his throat. "Even so," he said, "I have to go by my list and you're not on it. I'll have to check with someone upstairs," he said, picking up the phone.

"Fair enough," said Robert, casually. "But we're supposed to perform at the board meeting, which ends in..." Robert looked at his watch theatrically, "...ten minutes. If you delay us and we miss it, I'll obviously have to let Mr Heron know why…"

The security guard put the phone down. He knew how much Mr Heron liked magic, and if this kid was telling the truth, there'd be trouble if he'd stopped the show. "Okay," he said finally. "Take the express lift to the top floor. But, remember – no funny business or it's my neck on the line!"

Robert smiled and walked past the front desk towards the lift, with Chun Mai in tow. They pressed the button and waited.

"Remember, Chun Mai, big smiles for everyone," said Robert.

"Don't push your luck, Robert," replied Chun Mai.

As they stepped out of the lift, people stared. They were surprised to see two oddly-dressed children in their dull, grey workplace, but no one challenged them. They were sure that security wouldn't have let them in unless they were meant to be here. Robert marched confidently up to the door of the boardroom as Chun Mai trailed behind him with the crate.

"Are you ready, Chun Mai?" asked Robert, taking a deep breath.

"I suppose so," sighed Chun Mai.

"You remember all the tricks?" said Robert, a look of worry flitting across his face.

"Look, Robert, let's just get this over with and get out of here!" hissed Chun Mai.

Robert nodded and, with a flamboyant movement, he pushed the heavy boardroom doors open.

"Good morning, everyone!" he announced, as he strode into the room.

The room was filled with about twenty serious-looking men and women in suits. Seated at the head of the table was Heron, with his creepy assistant, Snidley. Robert was in his element; there was nothing he liked more than a room full of people looking straight at him.

"Hello, young man," said Heron, quietly. "Can I

help...?" he tailed off as he recognised Robert, "Wait," he said. "I know you! You're Roberto..."

"The *Great* Roberto," corrected Robert, striding to the front of the room, closely followed by Chun Mai. "I was asked by your staff to perform a surprise show for you. They know how much you love magic and wanted to congratulate you on the brilliant deal you pulled off yesterday, sir."

"How splendid! Yes, it was a great moment and the start of a whole new era," said Heron, smiling confidently, as his staff politely applauded him.

Snidley had noticed his boss's favourable reaction and rushed to take the credit. "That's right, sir," he said, "You've worked so hard to seal this contract that we thought you deserved a treat."

"How kind of you to arrange this for me at your own expense, Snidley," said Heron, smoothly.

"Oh, it was the least we could do," replied Snidley, wincing as he wondered just how much this 'Great Roberto' kid charged.

"Very well, young man!" said Heron, sitting back in his seat to watch the show. "I hear you're one of the best young magicians in the country. Show me what you can do!"

"I'll do my best," said Robert, shaking him by the hand. Then he clicked his fingers and a flame burst out of his hand. As the flames cleared, his audience gasped in amazement – in the split second that people were distracted by the flames, Robert had produced a large bouquet of flowers. He handed them to one of the female employees. "Beautiful flowers for a beautiful lady," he said, tipping his hat. The lady blushed as the boardroom erupted into a round of applause.

"One of my favourites," said Heron, laughing. "But I know how that one's done. Paraffin up your sleeves to make the fire and the flowers were in your jacket. Come on, show me something else...something more exciting," urged Heron, encouragingly.

"Before we continue..." said Robert, calmly, "do you have the time, Mr Heron?"

Heron looked down at his wrist, only to find his gold watch missing. He laughed. "The old missing watch chestnut, eh?" he said, rolling his eyes. "Come on, Roberto. Show me some new tricks!"

Chun Mai smiled as she produced the shiny watch. Robert had taken it when he shook Heron's hand, and thrown it to her as everyone watched the fireball. Smiling, Heron took the watch from Chun Mai and fastened it around his wrist. He would have been far more concerned if he'd realised what else Robert had taken from him during that handshake. Chun Mai was also holding his mobile phone behind her back. She wandered over to the window, waited until Robert sent three live doves flapping out of his hat and quickly dropped the phone out of the window while everybody was distracted.

The phone fell one floor to a strategically placed window-cleaning platform where Jake was waiting with a net.

He smiled as he deftly caught the phone and wired it up to his laptop. Soon the contents of the phone were downloading on to the computer.

Back in the boardroom, Heron was growing fidgety. All the tricks that Robert was showing him were too easy – he'd heard The Great Roberto was a brilliant magician, but so far all he'd shown him were basic tricks. Chun Mai could tell that he was beginning to get bored. Would Heron throw them out before Jake had a chance to get the phone back to her?

"You're losing his attention!" Chun Mai whispered to Robert, as she handed him one of the employees' laptops so that he could make it vanish. Robert simply ignored her – he knew what he was doing. Besides, he was in performance mode now! As Robert made the laptop disappear into thin air, Chun Mai rushed over to the window and signalled frantically to Jake that she needed the phone back. Unfortunately, it hadn't finished downloading.

"Right. It's time for a card trick now," said Robert.

"A card trick?" said Heron, raising an eyebrow. "I do hope you're not going to insult me with anything too basic!"

Robert merely smiled. "Think of a card, Mr Heron," he instructed.

Heron nodded as Chun Mai subtly gestured out of the window to Jake. Jake looked at the download in progress box on the computer screen, ninety per cent complete… ninety-five. "Come on, come on!" he muttered, impatiently.

"Ala…kazam!" cried Robert, throwing his arms out in front of him and firing hundreds of cards out of his sleeves across the boardroom. As the employees looked around, they noticed something odd. All the cards were the same. Every single one was the seven of spades.

Meanwhile, out on the platform, Jake had just completed the download. He chucked the phone back through the window and it fell at Chun Mai's feet with a light thud. She picked it up quickly.

"Is that your card Mr Heron?" asked Robert. He already knew that it was. Heron was stunned. This was great! He had to find out how it was done. Heron loved the way magicians could fool people with some simple trickery. Still, he mused; it wasn't a patch on his own magic show, being played out in Downing Street. At this very moment the entire country was being taken in by Rufus Heron's spectacular illusion – the fake Prime Minister. Now that was a brilliant trick.

Snapping his attention back to Robert, Heron smiled. "Well, my boy. Just when I had begun to think you were a dud," he grinned. "We must have a chat, so you can tell me how you do that…"

"It's all just simple magic!" said Robert, winking. Hearing Robert's coded signal, Jake dialled Robert's mobile. Robert picked it up and had a brief, pretend conversation. "I'm so sorry, Mr Heron, I'm afraid our chat will have to wait. That was my agent. I've got an interview with Magic Magazine in half an hour, so I'm afraid we will have to get going."

Chun Mai was panicking. She still had Heron's phone and Robert was wrapping up the show. How was she going to get it back into Heron's pocket without him noticing? There was only one thing for it!

"Mr Heron, I think you're wonderful! Well done for getting the Future Cities contract," she said, running up to Heron and hugging him tightly.

"Oh, err...thank you, young lady," managed Heron, slightly thrown by Chun Mai's sudden enthusiasm. Chun Mai quickly slipped the phone back into his pocket, then turned on her heel and hurried out of the door with Robert.

A short while later they found themselves back in the street.

Chun Mai glared at Robert, "Ugh! I can't believe I had to hug him, Robert. That was gross. You owe me, big time!"

9
a setback

As soon as the kids were all back in Sarah's room, Robert was shamelessly bragging to Alex and Sarah. He was full of stories about how he'd just performed a brilliant magic show. Hearing him boast, you'd have thought that he had single-handedly copied the phone data that would help them save Jonathan. Chun Mai and Jake kept quiet. When Robert was in full flow there was little point in arguing with him.

Using the downloaded information, the kids had been able to clone Heron's mobile phone. As soon as Heron made or received a call, it would show up on Jake's laptop. More importantly, they'd all be able to listen in.

"How do we know he'll even say anything about the PM on the phone?" asked Jake. "He doesn't strike me as the type that would do his own dirty work. I bet he's got other people to handle the kidnapping for him."

"I doubt it. My guess is that he wouldn't want to get too many people involved in something as big as this. They might talk," said Sarah. "I'm sure he'll be handling it himself. Sooner or later he'll say something that will lead us to Jonathan," she added, trying to convince herself as much as Jake.

"Well, either way, I guess we'll know soon enough," added Alex.

The kids stared at the laptop expectantly.

WHAT HAPPENS NEXT? YOU DECIDE...

A tough call

turn to page 106

Mousebug

turn to page 113

a TOUGH CALL

It wasn't long before the first call came in. The kids held their breath as they heard a ringing noise from the laptop's speaker. There was a click, followed by a woman's voice.

"Good morning, Mr Heron."

"Rebecca," replied Heron. "Can you organise a car for me and pick up my dry cleaning?" he instructed.

"Will do, sir," said Rebecca. With that, the line went dead. The kids all looked at each other, more than a little disappointed.

"Well, that wasn't much help," said Robert. "All we've found out is that he's going out and he'll be wearing a clean suit!"

"That's just one call," replied Sarah. "You need to be patient, Robert."

The kids waited by the laptop for the rest of the morning. Calls kept coming in, but they were all really dull. All Heron seemed to do was have long, boring conversations with his employees or ring up his secretary to give her menial jobs. He didn't once mention the Prime Minister, or the Future Cities.

After listening in on yet another of Heron's tedious calls, this time about a round of golf, Robert said what everyone was thinking, "This is getting us nowhere."

"We just need to be patient," said Sarah, hopefully. "He'll say something useful eventually, I know it."

"But that's the problem. We don't know how much time we've got," said Jake. "What if he's going to get rid of Jonathan...permanently?"

"I know," she sighed, "But how else can we find out where he is?"

"We call a guy who knows," replied Jake, grinning.

The rest of the group looked at him, confused. "I don't follow," said Sarah. "The only person who knows is Heron..."

"Chun Mai, we can make calls with the computer, right?" asked Jake.

"Of course," said Chun Mai. "It's a complete clone of Heron's phone."

"And if we do, it'll look like it's Heron calling from his mobile?"

"Yep," said Chun Mai, nodding.

"Then we call that Snidley bloke," said Jake. "He's Heron's right-hand man, yeah? Sarah, you said yourself that he was there at the presentation when this was all being planned, right? So, we can get his number from Heron's contact list on the phone and give him a call."

"Good plan, Jake" said Alex, "There's just one problem. As soon as we start speaking, Snidley's going to know we're not Heron!"

"I know," said Jake, smiling. "That's where Sarah comes in."

As well as being a languages expert, Sarah was also an excellent mimic. She did hilarious impressions of celebrities, as well as the kids and even Julian. So far, though, she had only really done it as a bit of fun, to make her friends laugh.

"Come on," said Sarah, "It's one thing to mess about mimicking you guys, but I won't fool Snidley, he speaks to Heron every day. He knows him too well."

"I think you can do it, Sarah!" said Chun Mai. "Your impression of me is spot on."

"Yeah, but this is completely different," replied Sarah, with a worried look on her face. "The plan's too risky."

"But at the moment it's the only plan we have and time's running out, Sarah," said Alex, gently.

Sarah frowned; he was right. She took herself off to a secluded part of HQ and watched some of Heron's speeches that Chun Mai had found on the Heron Construction website. She winced as she listened to the deep, confident tone of his voice. It would be a real struggle for her young voice to match it. Finally, after she'd practised over and over again, her impression was as good as it could be. Sarah took a deep breath and went back to her room, where the rest of the kids were waiting.

"Ready?" asked Chun Mai when she saw Sarah.

"As ready as I'll ever be!" replied Sarah in what sounded, to the kids at least, like a perfect impression of Heron's voice. The kids laughed and clapped enthusiastically but Sarah was far too nervous to crack a smile.

"That's brilliant, Sarah," said Robert.

"It'd fool me!" added Chun Mai.

"But it's not you I need to fool," said Sarah. "I have to convince Heron's most trusted employee."

The kids nodded. There was no question – this was going to be really tricky. Chun Mai plugged a small microphone into the laptop. "You need to speak into this," she said.

"Really? I never would have guessed," said Sarah sarcastically. Her nerves were making her irritable.

Alex handed Sarah a scrap of paper with Snidley's phone number on it. Sarah took a breath and tried to stop her hand shaking as she tapped it into the keyboard.

"Good luck," mouthed Jake.

After a couple of rings, Snidley answered.

"Yes, Mr Heron?" came Snidley's creepy voice through the laptop speaker.

"Where are you?" said Sarah, mimicking Heron's smooth, confident tone.

"I'm on the billionaire – just arrived," he replied.

Chun Mai feverishly wrote down the word 'billionaire.' What on earth does that mean? she wondered. How could he be on a billionaire?

"And Holmes?" Sarah asked.

The kids crossed their fingers hopefully. There was a long pause before Snidley responded. "Well, naturally, Sir, he's here too," he replied, finally.

Jake punched the air in delight. The Prime Minister was alive!

"Sir, if I may ask...I thought you said we weren't to mention that over the phone," continued Snidley.

Sarah had to remain focused. She was aware that she'd slipped up by asking so blatantly about Jonathan. Snidley was becoming suspicious.

"Yes I did," she said calmly into the phone. "That was a test, Snidley, to make sure you understood my instructions. Clearly you didn't!"

"I'm very sorry, Sir..."

"Let's move on, Snidley," replied Sarah. "Is everything else going according to plan, at least?" she asked.

"Do you really want me to answer that, Sir?"

"Of course I do," said Sarah, sharply.

"All's well, Sir. We're on schedule to start phase two later today," said Snidley.

Chun Mai was frantically taking notes. They needed to find out exactly what was happening later!

"Very good, Snidley," said Sarah, but as she did her voice slipped a little. Sarah froze in fear.

"Sir, is everything okay?" asked Snidley, suspicion creeping into his voice.

Chun Mai gestured to Sarah to end the call.

"Yes, yes," blustered Sarah. "I've just got a sore throat," she added abruptly, ending the call.

Nobody said anything for a minute. The phone call had been interesting to say the least, but it had left the kids with more questions than answers. What was happening later today? What could this 'phase two' that Snidley had mentioned be? And what on earth was 'the billionaire'? Was it a code? Was it a place?

At least there was no doubt about one thing: Heron had Jonathan Holmes and they had to get him back. Preferably before 'phase two' was put into operation...

Now continue to page 119

mousebug

Ever the good host, Sarah had provided a jug of fruit juice, in case anyone needed a drink while they were plotting in her room. Alex, bored of waiting for a call to come in, was pouring himself a big glass. Espionage, it turned out, was thirsty work. As usual, Alex's shoelaces were flapping about, untied. Alex was so scatter-brained that he often forgot to tie them, or even notice that they were trailing as he walked. On his way back over to the computer, he caught one with his right foot and tripped.

As he tumbled to the floor, the glass flew out of his hand. The kids watched as it shot across the room and came crashing down on the open laptop. The fruit juice flooded the keyboard and, with a sudden pffff, the screen went blank. Their only hope of finding the Prime Minister had just been washed away.

"Oh, drat," said Alex, wincing.

Chun Mai sighed, Sarah bit her fist in frustration, Robert put his head in his hands and Jake said some rude words under his breath. Finally, after what seemed like an eternity, Robert spoke.

"Jake," he said, "Please tell me that you backed up the information we got off the phone." Jake shook his head. "Alex, you moron!" exploded Robert. "Why can't you tie your shoelaces like everyone else?"

"Hey!" said Chun Mai, protectively. "It was an accident. It could have happened to anyone."

"No, Chun Mai, it's okay. Robert's right. I'm a moron," said Alex, getting up off the floor. "I've ruined everything. We'll never find the Prime Minister now."

Alex looked devastated, as if he was about to cry at any moment. Chun Mai patted him reassuringly on the shoulder. "That was our only lead!" he added, biting back tears.

"Not quite," said Chun Mai. The kids all turned to look at her hopefully. "There is something else, but it's a long shot."

"Well, don't keep us in suspense," said Robert.

"The mousebug," said Chun Mai. "I thought we needed a back-up plan in case the magic show didn't work – no offence Robert," she said, winking. "So I borrowed it and dropped it in Heron's boardroom this morning. I hope you don't mind, Alex?"

"Mind? Of course I don't mind," said Alex, the colour returning to his cheeks instantly. "Chun Mai, that's so brilliant, I could kiss you!"

"Don't you dare!" replied Chun Mai, but Alex didn't hear. He had already hurried out of Sarah's room. A few minutes later he returned with the mousebug's remote control.

"Can you remember where you put it, Chun Mai?" asked Jake.

"It doesn't matter," interrupted Alex, excitedly. "The mousebug is programmed to find somewhere to hide close to the spot where it's dropped."

Alex tapped a small screen on the remote control. Through it, they could see images from a tiny camera in one of the mousebug's eyes. But at the moment there wasn't much to see. It was pitch black.

"We can't see a thing," moaned Robert.

"Don't worry, that's because it's probably hidden itself behind the skirting boards. Look, I'll switch the night-vision on."

With just a few taps, the screen was filled with a green-tinged image. Alex was right – the mousebug had crawled behind the skirting boards. Slowly and carefully, Alex manoeuvred it along the long, dark, dusty insides of the wall until the mousebug finally reached a tiny hole.

"Chun Mai, I need a map of Heron Construction's HQ – fast!" he said.

"Way ahead of you," said Chun Mai, who had already called up the building's plans on her palmtop.

Alex returned to the joystick, frantically waggling it as he manoeuvred the mousebug down corridors and around corners, as Chun Mai sat beside him map-reading. Finally, the mousebug arrived at what should have been Heron's office door. Alex sat back, waiting for something.

"What is it?" said Robert, impatiently. "Why have you stopped?"

"The mousebug may be advanced Robert, but it can't open doors," replied Alex.

"Oh," muttered Robert, feeling a little foolish.

"Not yet, anyway," added Alex with a grin.

Suddenly he sat up with a jolt, as he saw two legs walking towards the camera. He pointed the mousebug's head upwards. It was Heron! Alex waited until Heron had pushed open the office door, then quickly manouevred the mouse inside the room. Then he carefully steered the mousebug behind a plant pot, so that only its face was visible. The kids watched as Heron walked towards his desk and began dialling a number on the phone.

"He's making a phone call, Alex!" said Chun Mai. "Can we listen in?"

"One sec," said Alex, pressing a button on the remote control. A small antenna rose up from the mousebug's back and pointed towards the phone. "Now we can."

The kids breathed a deep sigh of relief as they

heard Heron's voice coming through the speaker on the side of the remote control.

"Snidley," said Heron, quietly. "It's me."

"Bingo!" said Alex, smiling.

Luckily, Heron was using hands-free mode, so the kids could hear both sides of the conversation.

"Are you at the agreed location?" asked Heron.

"Yes Sir, I'm on the billionaire," said Snidley.

"I told you, no names!" snapped Heron. "Is our guest comfortable?"

"He must mean Jonathan!" said Sarah, clapping her hands. "He's alive!"

"No more than is strictly necessary," replied Snidley, with a creepy laugh.

Heron laughed coldly, "Good, good. Be ready for phase two of our little plan later today," he added, hanging up.

"Not one for in-depth conversations, Heron, is he?" said Robert as the kids looked at each other, now more confused than ever. What was 'phase two'? What was this plan about? And what was this 'billionaire' he talked about? Was it a code? Was it a place?

"At least there's no doubt about one thing any more," said Jake, "Heron definitely has the Prime Minister."

"And we're the only people who can rescue him," added Robert.

"By the sounds of it, we've only got a few hours. We need to find him before they start 'phase two', whatever that is," said Sarah.

"No pressure, then," sighed Chun Mai.

10

THE BILLIONAIRE

Meanwhile, Jonathan Holmes was feeling confused. He'd been drifting in and out of consciousness for what seemed like days now, but this was the first time he had been fully awake. He was hungry, thirsty and he had a pounding headache. He noticed with concern that his hands were tied behind his back. What on earth was going on, he wondered and where was he? One thing was certain – he was in trouble.

Jonathan looked around the room for some clues to try to piece together what had happened. He was in a dank, dingy utility room of some sort. A life jacket was lying on the floor and there were several maps pinned to the wall. He thought he could hear seagulls, too. As he took in more of his surroundings, Jonathan had the strangest sensation. The floor seemed to be bobbing up and down – he must be on a boat.

An open doorway in front of him was the only

urce of light, and silhouetted against it was a thin, shadowy figure. It was vaguely familiar.

"Hello, Prime Minister," said the figure.

"Who are you?" replied Jonathan, fiercely.

"Tut, tut. You're really not in a position to speak to me in that tone of voice, Prime Minister," said the figure, smugly. "We're in charge now, so I suggest you be careful. If you had taken our advice about the Future Cities you wouldn't be here."

"Seymour Snidley," said Jonathan in disdain as he recognised Heron's odious right-hand man.

Snidley flicked on the light to reveal his thin face. Anger began to pulse through Jonathan, his cheeks burned red with rage as the events of the past few days came flooding back. The last thing he'd seen before he passed out had been Heron's gleeful face. It was not an image he was likely to forget in a hurry.

"Got it in one, Holmes," grinned Snidley.

"So where's Heron? Is he too cowardly to do his own dirty work?" said Jonathan, sarcastically.

"Mr Heron has delegated this part of the task to me," responded Snidley with a thin smile.

Although Jonathan was doing his best to hide it, he felt *very* scared. He was tied up in a strange place and who knew what this Snidley character was going to do? But he was determined that Snidley wouldn't see that he was frightened, no matter what happened. He took a breath. "If you're going to kill me, get it over with!" he said, boldly.

Snidley gave a small, humourless snigger. "Kill you?" he said. "We're not going to do that. In fact, this time tomorrow you'll be back in Downing Street. No one will ever know you were gone."

"What?" spluttered Jonathan, more bewildered than ever.

"It's very simple, Prime Minister," said Snidley. "We have installed a very convincing Jonathan Holmes double at Downing Street."

"You've done *what*?" yelled the Prime Minister in

fury. "No one will ever believe that it's me!"

"Actually, they've all been taken in," said Snidley, grinning. "Once we've corrected your little error over the Future Cities contract, you'll be going home. It's too important to us for you to get in our way. Tomorrow your stand-in will sign the contract, then we'll take you back," added Snidley, airily.

"The minute I'm back, I'll tear it up and have you and Heron arrested!" shouted Jonathan.

"Calm down, Prime Minister," said Snidley. "Heron Construction has the finest lawyers money can buy. Trust me, the contracts are water-tight, and as far as arresting us goes…for what exactly? You can't prove a thing!"

"I'll find a way, Snidley," replied Jonathan, grimly. "You won't get away with this!"

"But no one will believe you. That's the beauty of the plan. It's too far-fetched. If you start spouting off about conspiracies and secret abductions, they'll all think you've gone completely bonkers."

"You snivelling little…" began Jonathan.

"The best thing for you to do, Holmes, is to go back to Downing Street and keep your mouth shut," said Snidley. "It's a shame it had to come to this. If you'd signed the contract, Mr Heron would've made sure you were handsomely rewarded."

With that, Snidley marched out of the door and left Jonathan alone.

"Snidley!" shouted Jonathan Holmes. "Come back here at once!"

While the Prime Minister was having this unpleasant encounter, back at M.I.Five HQ, there were problems, too. Chun Mai had hacked into the Downing Street server and accessed the fake Prime Minister's schedule – worryingly, it hadn't taken her long at all. In there, a meeting was marked for 4pm that afternoon. It was labelled 'Signing Future Cities contract with Rufus Heron.'

"That must be 'phase two'," sighed Chun Mai. "Once the fake Prime Minister has signed that contract, Heron will get to build his cities."

"So we have to rescue Jonathan before the meeting?" said Jake, glancing at the clock on the wall. They didn't have long.

"Spot on, Jake," said Alex, looking worried.

"It's unlikely," said Robert. "Seeing as we don't even know where he's being held hostage! He could be anywhere!"

"Well, Snidley said he was 'on the billionaire', didn't he?" said Alex. "That must mean something."

"I bet it's a code," said Jake.

"But code for what?" asked Sarah, gloomily.

"I don't know," admitted Jake. "It's so vague we can't even guess!"

Chun Mai idly tapped a button on her laptop and replayed the recording of the phone conversation with Snidley. It felt like the thousandth time they'd heard it, but maybe they'd missed something...Sarah rolled her eyes as Heron's voice filled the room yet again. "Oh, turn it off Chun Mai," she said. "I don't want to hear his smarmy voice again."

"No, wait!" yelled Jake, noticing something. He rushed over to Chun Mai. "Play that last bit again!" he demanded. "There's something in the background," he added, excitedly. "Can you cut out some of the interference, Chun Mai?"

She hadn't heard anything, but to humour Jake she tapped a couple of keys and played it again. To her amazement, he was right. This time she heard what Jake was talking about. Very faintly in the background they could hear the sound of a horn.

"That's a boat!" said Jake, confidently.

The rest of the kids looked at him; they weren't completely convinced. "Are you sure about that, Jake?" asked Sarah.

"Yeah," said Chun Mai. "It could just as easily be a car horn or an alarm..."

"I'd bet money on it," said Jake.

"Since when are you such a marine expert?" said Robert. "I thought you were a city boy."

"I am, but I used to spend every summer with my uncle in Cornwall. We did loads of sea fishing and that's a boat horn for sure. So Snidley must have been near a boat, which means that..."

"The Prime Minister's being held by the sea!" cut in Sarah. "Chun Mai, check through Heron's records. See if he owns any harbours or docks – anything that could be relevant."

Chun Mai began to type at top speed as the others gazed anxiously over her shoulder. Eventually she sighed. "Sorry, Jake. It doesn't look as if he owns anything like that. Are you sure it wasn't just a…"

"What about boats?" interrupted Robert, with a flash of inspiration. "Rich people love splashing their cash on those! My dad's got three…"

Chun Mai ignored Robert's bragging and tapped away at her keyboard. "Yes!" she shouted.

"What is it, Chun Mai?" asked Sarah. "Does Heron have a boat?"

"Yes he does," replied Chun Mai, grinning from ear to ear. "And you'll never guess what it's called!"

"Well, don't keep us in suspense!" cried Robert.

"The Billionaire!" crowed Chun Mai.

The kids went wild. They leapt about high-fiving each other. It wasn't code at all! Heron was talking about his boat. Finally, they knew where the Prime Minister was being held.

"Well done, guys!" said Sarah. "But we still have a lot to do." The kids calmed down. "Where's this 'Billionaire' moored?" asked Sarah, keeping her fingers crossed that it wasn't in Australia.

"Monaco," replied Chun Mai.

"Well, I guess we're going to Monaco then," said Sarah, grinning.

"Come on, let's go!" said Jake jumping out of his chair. He bounded out of Sarah's room, followed closely by the rest of the kids.

As soon as they got into the hallway, they stopped abruptly. Julian, together with three serious-looking men in uniform, was blocking their path.

"Just a moment!" said Julian. The kids turned pale. Why did he have to show up now, just when they were getting somewhere?

Jake sighed. Julian's tone of voice told him that this was more than just bad luck, he knew something was up. "Where do you think you're going?" demanded Julian. Jake suspected he already knew the answer to that question.

"We're following up a lead," said Sarah.

"I told you to take the day off, Agent Moore," said Julian, ominously. "I don't suppose this would have anything to do with Rufus Heron, would it?" he asked, raising an eyebrow.

"Of course not, Agent Morris," said Chun Mai. "You told us not to investigate him."

"I'm glad you remember that conversation, Chun Mai," said Julian. "Perhaps you can explain this?"

Julian thrust a piece of paper into Sarah's hand. It was a list of websites and computer servers that Chun Mai had visited, plus a note of the telephone numbers that they'd called.

"We've been monitoring all of you today, after last night's debacle," he said, quietly.

Julian was fierce and barked orders when it came to day-to-day stuff, but when they were in really big trouble he was extremely calm and controlled. It was very, very unnerving to be on the wrong side of him when he was like this and the kids knew that at this moment he was beyond furious.

"You've defied orders yet again," said Julian.

"We're sorry, Julian," said Jake. "But we had..."

"Enough, Jake!" said Julian. "No more excuses. At least when Sarah was kidnapped you were trying, in a misguided way, to help a fellow agent. But this, this witch hunt shows me..."

"It's not a witch hunt," interrupted Sarah. "Julian, you have to believe us. Rufus Heron has kidnapped Jonathan Holmes..."

"Sarah, I've had quite enough of your mad stories to last me a lifetime," snapped Julian.

"Julian, please, you've got to believe us," begged Sarah, desperately.

"Sarah," said Julian, holding up his finger to silence her. "I don't want to hear another word. Your recent antics have come to the attention of MI6 bosses. They are deeply unhappy that you insulted the PM last night. Now you've been harassing businessmen today, too. I have been instructed to hand you over to these military policemen. You'll be escorted to a holding cell while they make a decision about your future here. They want to be sure you can't cause any further embarrassment while your fate is being decided."

"You can't put us in a cell!" cried Robert, aghast. "Just what are we supposed to have done?"

"Insubordination, disobeying direct orders, misuse of MI6 facilities, insulting the PM" said Julian. "Not to mention the unauthorised computer hacking," he added, looking sternly at Chun Mai.

"But what's going to happen to us?" asked Alex, looking scared.

"I doubt you will be staying with MI6," said Julian, pausing as the kids struggled to take this in. As he looked at their shattered expressions, he softened slightly. In spite of everything, deep down he had grown fond of them. He was sad that it had come to this, but orders were orders and the kids had disobeyed them yet again. "I'll try to make sure you don't face criminal charges, but I can't promise anything," he added finally. "Take them away, officers."

The military policemen advanced on the kids and grabbed one in each arm.

"Julian, wait!" shouted Sarah as she was led away. "You have to believe us. The man in Downing Street is an impostor. Jonathan Holmes is being held on a boat in Monaco!" Sarah continued to shout until Julian was well out of earshot, before allowing herself to be led away forlornly.

The kids were taken outside. Presumably they were going to a police station or a secure building. Sarah sighed; by the time they were released it would be too late to do anything about the fake Prime Minister. The deal would be done and Heron's dangerous cities would be built. It was unbearable to be so close to rescuing Jonathan!

Suddenly, a radio crackled into life. It belonged to the guard who was holding Sarah and Jake. While he was briefly distracted by the incoming message, Sarah seized her chance. She stamped down as hard as she could on the guard's foot. It was enough to make him loosen his grip on her arm so that she could wriggle free. She sprinted away from the guard, to loud cheers from the other kids.

"Go, Sarah!" shouted Jake.

"She may be a bit girlie, but she's pretty speedy!" cried Chun Mai in delight.

"Oh, no you don't!" growled the guard. He couldn't chase after Sarah because he was still holding Jake, but he could make sure she didn't get out of the building. "Code red, secure the exits!" he shouted into his radio.

11
SOLO MISSION

Sarah sprinted down the hallway as fast as she could. Alarms were going off all around her. She had about thirty seconds before the metal security doors would descend, blocking all of the exits. Up until now, she had liked the fact that the M.I.Five HQ was such a secure building – she'd never imagined that one day she'd need to escape.

I've got to get up to the roof, she thought as she leapt up the stairs three at a time and sprinted past the bedrooms. At the foot of the top flight she could see the security door was starting to close. With a final burst of energy, she ran up the stairs and dived under the metal door, flicking the handle as she went. Thankfully, the back door opened and Sarah rolled out on to the roof. She looked back as the heavy steel door closed tight and breathed a sigh of relief. She'd made it!

Sarah hurried over to the hoverpod hangar and pressed her finger against the fingerprint reader. The hangar door slid open – she was relieved to see Julian hadn't managed to cancel her security access yet. As she hopped into a hoverpod seat, Sarah realised with panic that she'd never actually flown one before. She'd only watched Jake and Robert. Oh well, she thought, strapping herself in tight, it's too late to worry about it now. She looked down at the dashboard wondering how on earth to start the engine.

Her thoughts were rudely interrupted by a loud shout from the other end of the hangar, "Stop right there!" It was Julian. He must have guessed she'd try to use a hoverpod to escape. "Get out of the hoverpod, Sarah," he commanded.

"Sorry, Julian. You won't listen, so I have no choice!" replied Sarah.

"Sarah, that was not a request, it was an order," barked Julian. He looked furious!

Sarah wasn't about to start listening to orders now, not when she was the only person who could stop Heron and save the Prime Minister. Julian would have to wait.

"I'd step aside if I were you, Julian," she said, as she thumped a button marked 'Ignition'.

To her delight, the hoverpod roared into life and lurched forwards. Julian was forced to duck as the machine soared over his head and scraped the hangar door before zooming off into the sky. It didn't take Sarah long to figure out the controls. First of all, she found the camouflage function and switched it on so that she wouldn't be seen. Then, after a couple of near misses with some skyscrapers, she headed south. Her solo mission had started.

Sarah flew over France as fast as she dared, and in less than two hours she spotted the sparkling waters of the Mediterranean Sea.

She'd reached Monaco. She parked the hoverpod behind a fancy restaurant next to the Monte Carlo Marina and, pausing only to grab the remote control, hurried off to search for Heron's boat.

Monaco is home to hundreds of people who have one thing in common – they are all unbelievably wealthy. Sarah's heart dropped as she looked at the marina. Just as Robert had pointed out earlier, rich people certainly loved buying boats. Everywhere she looked there was row upon row of enormous yachts. It would take Sarah far too long to check the names. She needed a faster way to find the 'The Billionaire.'

She saw a large building with a sign over the door which said, 'Manager's Office' in French. Sarah smiled as a plan began to form in her mind. She ran into the pristine building and headed for the front desk. The well-groomed receptionist was startled to see a lone child approaching her. "Can I help you?" she said, in an irritated tone. She obviously didn't take kindly to children bustling into her stylish office.

"Can you help me? I've lost my parents," said Sarah in perfect French.

The woman frowned. "Well, what do you want me to do about it?" she replied in French, shrugging.

Sarah responded by bursting into floods of tears. "Please help me. The marina's so big – I wandered off and now I can't find them!" she said, covering her face to look as if she was sobbing uncontrollably.

The woman softened slightly. "Okay. I'll go and make an announcement over the loudspeaker," she said. "You wait here. Don't touch anything!"

"Oh, thank you," replied Sarah, pretending to be really grateful.

"I'll need your name," said the woman.

"Yes, err, it's Nicole, Nicole Laurent," replied Sarah, going with the first fake name that came to mind.

The snooty woman went into the back office to put out an announcement. As soon as she left, Sarah sprang into action. She ran behind the desk and rummaged through the neat piles of papers until she found a black book. 'Bingo!' she thought. It was a record of all the boats that were berthed in the marina. Sarah flicked back through the dates to the day after Jonathan was kidnapped. Just as she had expected, that's when The Billionaire had arrived. It was moored in berth 116, at the far end of the marina. Sarah smiled and hurried out of the door, moments before the French woman reappeared.

When she got to berth 116, Sarah was relieved to find The Billionaire bobbing up and down, but worryingly, it seemed that the crew were getting it ready for a trip. A large crate containing fuel, water and food sat on the jetty, waiting to be loaded on board by a mechanical winch. Sarah waited until the crew were busy, then crept over to the crate. She hopped inside and covered herself with a heavy tarpaulin.

After a few minutes she felt the crate being lifted off the ground. Then there was a slight jolt as it was placed on to the deck. It was hot and stuffy, and the smell of diesel was overpowering, but Sarah didn't care. She had made it on to The Billionaire! Not long after, Sarah felt the boat moving. She peeked out from underneath the tarpaulin. The crew were milling around, but there didn't seem to be much going on. As soon as she was sure that no one was looking, she slipped silently out of the crate and edged along the deck.

Sarah carefully opened the door leading below deck and walked softly down the stairs. She assumed that was where Jonathan would be held and she was right. As she walked along the corridor, she heard voices coming from one of the rooms. Sarah pressed her ear against the thin wooden door. She could hear every word of the conversation on the other side.

"Where are we going, Snidley?" demanded one of the voices.

Sarah smiled. It was Jonathan Holmes!

"Nowhere in particular, Prime Minister. We're just taking a little trip until the contract has been signed," replied Snidley. "Consider it an additional security measure – not that we expect you to escape, of course," he added, laughing nastily.

Now she'd found the Prime Minister, all Sarah had to do was get him off the boat…

WHAT HAPPENS NEXT? YOU DECIDE...

Sarah and Jonathan take the plunge
turn to page 140

Sarah takes the helm
turn to page 144

Sarah and Jonathan Take the Plunge

Sarah crept back along the corridor towards the steps. She had to formulate a plan – fast! What she needed was something to distract the crew. Just then a solution presented itself. Attached to the wall was a grey metal box with 'Flare gun – Emergencies only!' stamped on it. She opened the box and grabbed it.

Flare guns fire cartridges that explode, leaving a brightly-coloured cloud in the sky. They're used as distress signals, but that wasn't what Sarah was going to use it for. What she was going to do was a little crazier, dangerous even, but at this point she had no other choice. Creeping on to the deck, she closed her eyes and fired the flare gun at the bridge. The cartridge exploded with an almighty bang, sending red smoke billowing into the control room.

Sarah ducked behind the crate and waited. She knew the noise and huge cloud of smoke was going to send Snidley and the crew into a panic. That was what she was counting on. Seconds later, the entire crew was hurrying upstairs to the bridge, joined by Snidley, who must have heard the bang from below deck.

"Which one of you clowns let the flare gun off?" he demanded, angrily.

Each member of the crew proceeded to protest their innocence and soon chaos had descended as they all shouted at once. Amongst all the noise, confusion and thick red smoke, Sarah was able to run downstairs unseen.

In the confusion, Snidley had left the door to the Prime Minister's room slightly ajar. Sarah grinned as she pushed it open and ran in.

"Sarah?" said Jonathan in shock. "What are you doing here?"

"Shh!" said Sarah, anxious that they would be overheard. "I'm saving you," she whispered, as she loosened the ropes around his hands and feet. As soon as the knots were untied, Sarah led Jonathan carefully back up the stairs to the main deck. The smoke had thinned slightly but the argument between Snidley and the crew was still in full swing.

"When I say run, go to the bow," said Sarah, pointing towards the front of the boat. Jonathan nodded as Sarah watched the crew, waiting for the right moment. Once she was sure that they were all distracted, she whispered, "Run!"

Sarah and Jonathan sped to the bow, undetected. She pulled the hoverpod remote control out of her pocket and pressed the 'Pick-up' button. The hoverpod rose silently from its hiding place behind the fancy restaurant, and shot off towards the boat.

"What have you got there?" asked Jonathan, pointing at the remote.

"You'll find out," said Sarah, frantically.

Just then, they heard shouting. "Oi! What's your game?" said the voice. It was the boat's captain. He'd spotted them from the bridge, which was now clear of smoke. Sarah felt a wave of panic rising as he pulled out a walkie-talkie to call Snidley. In a few moments they would be caught.

Sarah climbed over the boat's safety rail and gestured for Jonathan to do the same. He followed her tentatively.

"We have to jump, Jonathan," said Sarah.

"Umm...I'm not really sure that's a good idea..." said the Prime Minister anxiously, as he eyed the choppy waters far below.

"We have no choice!" said Sarah, urgently.

Out of the corner of her eye, Sarah could see Snidley and the rest of the crew hurrying towards them. There was no time to lose, but Jonathan seemed to be frozen to the spot.

"Prime Minister?" began Sarah.

"Yes, Sarah?" he said, nervously.

"Sorry!" she shouted, pushing him off the side of the boat, then jumping in after him.

They gasped as they crashed into the cold water, spluttering as they surfaced. To Sarah's huge relief, she spotted the hoverpod speeding towards them underwater. As the strange machine rose up out of the waves, Jonathan gasped with surprise. Sarah bundled him inside, then leapt in beside him, as the hoverpod zoomed off into the sky. Sarah couldn't resist giving Snidley a cheeky wave as they blazed past him on their way back to London.

Now continue to page 151

Sarah Takes
The Helm

The boat had only been moving for about ten minutes
when Sarah noticed with surprise that the engines had
stopped. She needed to do something. As she stood
outside the door of the cabin, she could hear two of
the crew chatting. She crept upstairs to see what was
going on. One of the men looked really angry.

"Just leave it, mate!" said the first crew member,
an older man with tattoos all the way up his arms.
"You know what Heron's like. You don't wanna get on
the wrong side of him."

"Well, I've had it," said the other guy. "The pay's
lousy. We've been grafting non-stop for days. I want a
bigger wedge or I'm outta here."

Sarah looked across to the other end of the yacht,
where a lifeboat was clipped to the side. She smiled as

a plan began to form in her mind. Perfect! She waited until the men had walked away, then checked that the coast was clear. Edging around the deck, she let herself into what looked like an office. She rummaged around looking for a walkie-talkie, then stopped as she spotted something even better on the wall – the boat had an intercom system, so she could speak to the entire crew at once. Flicking the controls to 'Deck' so Snidley wouldn't hear, she took a deep breath and did what she hoped was a decent impression of him.

"Attention, crew!" she said. "Mr Heron has been very generous and left a little bonus on the boat. In the lifeboat you'll find a briefcase full of money. The first man there gets it!"

The crew looked at each other in confusion before they bolted to the back of the boat, shoving and pushing each other as they went. All five of them dived into the lifeboat, scrabbling around as they looked for the briefcase. They were so distracted by their greed that they didn't see Sarah press the 'Release' button. The lifeboat was almost in the water before they noticed, and by then it was too late. Sarah watched as the lifeboat drifted out to sea. "Catch you later, guys," she yelled, waving.

Below deck, Snidley was completely unaware of what was going on above him. A few minutes later he was rather puzzled to hear the boat's engines roaring into life.

"What's going on up there?" Snidley barked into the intercom. "Why are we moving?" he added. But there was no response. He headed up to the deck to see what was happening and got a huge shock. The boat was empty and the crew were gone! He ran to the front of the boat and looked up to the bridge. When he saw who was steering the boat, he was speechless. It was that wretched kid from the car park again.

"If you surrender now, I might let you live!" growled Snidley, with a nasty glint in his eye.

"Nice to see you too, Snidley," said Sarah. "But you know I don't give up that easily..." she laughed, pressing a button on the control panel.

Suddenly, Snidley heard the whirring noise of the anchor being lowered. He was confused until he looked down and realised what was happening. He was standing inside the thick coil of the anchor rope. As the rope began to spill over the side of the boat, it wound itself up around his waist. Snidley panicked, trying frantically to free himself, but it was no good and he found himself being dragged towards the side. Just as he was about to slip overboard, Sarah pressed the button again. The anchor ground to a halt, leaving Snidley pinned to the side of the boat by the thick rope.

"Get me out of here, right now, you horrible little freak!" screamed Snidley, thrashing from side-to-side.

"Sorry, Snidley. You're going nowhere!" replied Sarah with glee.

With Snidley well and truly dealt with, Sarah turned her attentions back to The Billionaire. According to the computer, they were about three miles away from the marina. At the current speed, she reckoned she had a couple of minutes to untie the Prime Minister before the boat got there. Sarah quickly tied a rope to the boat's wheel and fastened the other end to the window frame, hoping it would keep them on course. As she was leaving, a sudden wave pitched the boat sideways and she was briefly thrown off balance. She grabbed a handle to steady herself, but in her haste she hadn't noticed that it was the throttle – or that she had moved it to 'Maximum speed'.

Sarah raced below deck to get the Prime Minister. When she burst in through the door, Jonathan got the shock of his life.

"Sarah?" he spluttered. "What on earth are you doing here?"

"I'm saving you," she said matter-of-factly, as she quickly untied the ropes around his hands and feet.

"We don't have much time!" she said, hurrying to untie the last of the knots. "I'll explain later. Follow me," she said, rushing back out of the door. Jonathan did as he was told, glad that his ordeal was over. But it wasn't quite over yet. As they raced on to the deck, Sarah gasped in horror.

"Oh no! My calculations must have been wrong!" she cried as she saw that the boat was hurtling

towards the marina at full speed. There was no way that she'd stop it in time. "Quick, Jonathan, grab hold of something and get down," she yelled, throwing herself to the deck.

Seconds later, the boat ploughed into Monte Carlo Marina with a shattering roar. Wealthy boat owners screamed as it crashed and lurched along rows of expensive speedboats and yachts, demolishing jetties and pontoons in its wake. Sarah lost her grip on the railing and was thrown across the deck, hitting her head hard against the cabin wall. When the boat finally came to a rest, the marina was a complete wreck. Sarah opened one eye and winced as she peered at the chaos around her. "Are you okay, Jonathan?" she asked, in a small voice.

"Just about," replied Jonathan, in shock.

"Good. In that case, we'd better be off. The police will be arriving any second and I think we'll let Snidley take the rap for all this," she said, gesturing towards Heron's sidekick, who was still tangled in the anchor rope and now stuttering and white-faced with fear.

Jumping a few feet on to what was left of the marina, Sarah raced off to the hoverpod with a very puzzled Jonathan hurrying to keep up.

NOW CHOOSE YOUR ENDING!

A hairy moment
turn to page 152

Buying time
turn to page 162

Robert has a trick up his sleeve
turn to page 172

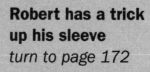

a Hairy moment

As they soared above Europe, Jonathan tried to get his head around the fact that he was being flown home by a twelve year-old in a weird, invisible machine. They had reached the English Channel before Sarah had explained everything to Jonathan.

"You have to come back to MI6 with me," said Sarah. "When you back up my story, then Julian will have to believe us!"

"I'd love to, Sarah, but we don't have time right now," said Jonathan, looking nervously at the ground as they approached London.

"What do you mean?" replied Sarah.

"Once that contract's signed this afternoon, my stand-in is going to disappear. Then there'll be no way to prove that it wasn't me who signed it. If that happens, Heron's cities will go ahead!"

Sarah frowned. It simply hadn't occurred to her

that once the fake Prime Minister had left, they'd have no evidence. "So what do you suggest?" she asked.

"There's only one thing for it," said Jonathan. "We have to go straight to Downing Street."

"What're you going to do?" asked Sarah, nervously.

"I'm going to get into that meeting and make them believe that I'm the genuine article," he said.

"Is that going to work?" asked Sarah, sceptically.

"I don't know," said Jonathan. "But we have to stop Heron, whatever it takes."

Sarah nodded. He was right. Desperate times call for desperate measures, she thought, ignoring the hoverpod's shuddering engine and accelerating up to top speed.

When they got to London, the closest place Sarah could find to land safely was a quiet corner of St James's Park. They hurriedly hid the hoverpod among some bushes, then sprinted off across the grass. Ordinary people don't expect to see their Prime Minister in person and when they do, they're surrounded by police and bodyguards. So the sight of Jonathan Holmes running through St James's Park, with only a young girl for company, caused a stir.

Sarah heard snippets of conversation as they ran past people.

"Oooh, look! Isn't that Jonathan Holmes?" said one old lady.

"Don't be daft! The Prime Minister wouldn't be

allowed to run round parks alone!" said her friend. "Besides, look at the state of him. Jonathan Holmes always looks immaculate!"

When they finally reached the security gate at Downing Street, Jonathan and Sarah were both out of breath. Jonathan looked through the bars at Paul, the security guard. "Paul, I know this looks...strange," he panted. "But I need you to let us in."

Because of the Prime Minister's unshaven face and dishevelled appearance, it took Paul a moment to recognise him. "Prime Minister?" he said, incredulously. "Is that really you?"

"Yes, Paul, it's really me," said Jonathan, wearily.

"But...you're already inside," replied Paul, with some confusion.

"I know, I know, it's very complicated. And I'm afraid I don't have the time to explain right now," said Jonathan, impatiently.

"He doesn't look anything like Jonathan Holmes!" said a tourist standing at the gate. Sarah glared as he shrugged and walked away.

"You know I can't just let you in," said Paul. "I wouldn't be doing my job if I did."

Jonathan sighed. "Okay. Your full name is Paul Cartwright. You have a wife called Cathy and two sons, Richard and James. Am I right?"

"Yes," replied Paul, suspiciously. "But anyone could find that out."

154

"Last Thursday, did I forget my pen on the way out and ask to borrow yours?"

"Yes," said Paul, feeling really confused now.

"Would I know that if I wasn't the Prime Minister?" demanded Jonathan, crossly.

"I suppose not," admitted Paul.

"Well, Paul, as Prime Minister I order you to open this gate!" said Jonathan, in an authoritative tone that Sarah hadn't heard before.

Any doubts that Paul had had were gone, instantly. This was the big boss alright! "Absolutely, Sir. Sorry, Sir," he said meekly, as the large metal gates slid open. Jonathan hurried through, followed by Sarah. The armed policeman at the front door picked up his radio and called inside for the door to be opened.

"Open up," he said. "It's the PM...I think!"

When Sue saw Jonathan, her jaw nearly hit the floor. "Prime Minister?" she asked, in amazement.

"Yes, Sue, before you ask, it really is me," replied Jonathan, brusquely.

"But, I've just seen...I mean...I saw you thirty seconds ago...upstairs with Mr Heron," she stammered, struggling to understand. "How did you out and get so...so...dirty?"

"I know this is hard to comprehend, Sue," sighed Jonathan. "I'll explain shortly, but first I have to get to that meeting with Heron."

"You want to go to a meeting you're already in?"

asked Sue, even more puzzled.

"Yes I do, Sue," said Jonathan, sympathising completely with her confusion. "Where is Heron?"

"He's in the White Drawing Room," she replied as Jonathan set off up the stairs.

Inside, the fake Prime Minister was about to sign the documents awarding the Future Cities contract to Heron. He was surrounded by various members of the government, all of whom were smiling and lining up to shake Heron's hand. Not one of them had even the faintest idea about the colossal mistake that they were about to make.

"This is truly a momentous day," boomed Henry, revelling in his role. "It is the begin…"

"Perhaps, Prime Minister, we should make our speeches *after* we've signed," said Heron, subtly raising his voice to tell Henry to get on with it.

"Oh...of course," said Henry, as Heron scrawled his signature across the paper and hurriedly thrust it back for Henry to sign. Just as Henry was picking up the pen, the heavy oak door crashed open. The assorted government officials gasped in shock as they stared at the real Jonathan Holmes, who was out of breath, red in the face and wearing a torn, filthy suit.

Henry blanched white with terror as he realised that he'd probably be going to jail. Heron however, wasn't prepared to give in quite so easily. "Who on earth is this?" he demanded, trying to appear calm and unruffled by this sudden and unexpected development.

"He's Jonathan Holmes, the real Prime Minister!" said Sarah, defiantly. "And you know exactly who I am, you had me kidnapped – remember?"

Heron looked coolly at Sarah. On the outside he looked perfectly calm, but inside he was panicking. What was the girl from the car park doing here? he wondered. He thought that Frankie had dealt with her.

"What on earth do you mean by all this, young lady?" interrupted Jeffrey Petersen, the Deputy Prime Minister, completely confused.

Jonathan answered for her. "Heron knew I'd never let him build the Future Cities, so he kidnapped me and put a look-alike in my place!" he said, angrily pointing at Henry. "I know it sounds crazy, but you have to trust me. I am the *real* Prime Minister!"

Heron snorted. "Is this some sort of practical joke?" he asked, calmly. He was going to have to do some fast talking to get out of this one. "Who would believe that anyone could execute such a ridiculous plan – especially me, of all people? I'm an honest and trustworthy businessman. Anyone can see this chap's off his head. Okay, he does look remarkably similar to Jonathan Holmes, but just look at the state of him!" he said, smoothly.

"Heron's quite right, this poor fellow's obviously deranged. Stay back, he could be dangerous!" said Henry, following Heron's lead. "I'll call security and have him taken away," he said, lifting the telephone.

The next moment, two burly policemen arrived. "Please arrest that man," said Henry, as calmly as he could manage. But he was panicking and his accent slipped for a moment. The policemen gave Henry an odd look, but did as they were told, grabbing Jonathan by the arms.

"Jeffrey," he shouted, frantically. "Can't you see? It's me, Jonathan."

"Make sure you arrest her, too," added Heron, pointing at Sarah. "Isn't it past your bedtime, little girl?" he asked, with a sarcastic smile.

Heron's words brought a memory flashing back into Sarah's mind. For a second she was back behind the bins at Banqueting House. The place where she'd first seen Heron talking to Henry about the plan. All she had seen of Henry was the back of his head...his bald head! As the thick arm of the policeman swooped towards her, she ducked and launched herself across the table at Henry. Before anyone could stop her, she grabbed a handful of his hair. The wig came straight off in her hand, leaving Henry as bald as a coot, with a room full of people staring at him in shock.

"I think you've got the wrong man, gentlemen," said Jeffrey to the policemen. "Arrest these two men immediately!"

Realising he was caught, Henry immediately started to blub. "I'm s-s-s-sorry...

I d-didn't want to…H-H-Heron threatened me!"

"Be quiet, you snivelling idiot," said Heron, quietly. "You'll regret this. My lawyers will sue the lot of you," he said, calmly as he was led away in handcuffs. But Heron would be in for a surprise – he wouldn't be able to sort this problem out with money.

When everyone had taken a moment to get over the shock of what had just happened, Jeffrey walked up to Jonathan and clapped him on the back. "Good to have you back, Prime Minister," he said, smiling.

"It's good to be back, Jeffrey," replied Jonathan, with a tired grin. It had been a long week.

"I can't believe we fell for it. I'm so sorry," said Jeffrey, feeling a little awkward.

"That's okay, Jeffrey. From what I gather he was very convincing. Thank goodness he didn't fool everyone," said Jonathan, grinning at Sarah. "Now, let's do the important bit," he added. Jonathan walked over to the other side of the table and picked up Heron's contract, "Actually, Sarah, would you like to do the honours?"

Sarah smiled as she tore the contract in half, and the room erupted in applause.

Now continue to page 188

Buying Time

Jonathan sat motionless, staring out of the hoverpod window. Sarah could see that he wasn't comfortable – he was gripping the sides of his seat so hard that his knuckles had turned white. Jonathan was finding it pretty hard to get his head round the fact that he was racing over Europe in an invisible flying machine piloted by a twelve-year-old girl.

As they thought about their next move, Jonathan explained to Sarah that the fake Prime Minister would 'disappear' after the contract was signed. They had to get to Downing Street before the signing, or there would be no way to prove what had gone on. The meeting with Heron was due to start in half an hour, which meant that they didn't have time for an elaborate plan. They would simply have to go to Number 10 and hope that Jonathan could persuade everyone that he was the real Prime Minister.

They were about twenty miles outside London when the hoverpod began to rattle and shake violently.

"Is that normal?" asked Jonathan, anxiously.

"I don't know," replied Sarah. "I've never flown one of these things before," she added, as Jonathan laughed nervously.

A sudden loud bang silenced them both, as Sarah struggled to control the hoverpod. Out of the corner of her eye she could see a cloud of thick black smoke pouring from one of the engines.

"I'm pretty sure that isn't normal!" she said, as Jonathan turned white with fear.

The hoverpod rapidly began to lose altitude and soon it was clear that they were going to have to crash-land. Sarah fought with the controls and did her best to aim for a field.

"Hold on tight!" she yelled frantically, but she needn't have bothered – Jonathan was clinging on to the edge of his seat so hard that he was in danger of ripping the fabric.

Sheep scattered as the hoverpod swooped down towards the field, smoke spewing from its engines. Sarah gripped the controls tightly and closed her eyes as the hoverpod ploughed into the ground. It skidded for what seemed like for ever, sending earth and bits of debris flying up into the air as it went. At last the hoverpod came to rest against a hedge. Sarah gingerly opened her eyes and looked across at Jonathan. He was clearly shaken, but not hurt. Sarah breathed a sigh of relief. They climbed out of the hoverpod and stood for a moment.

"Where do you think we are?" asked Jonathan.

"I don't know," replied Sarah. "But we won't make that meeting now!" she said, kicking the hoverpod in frustration.

"In that case, we're going to need to buy some time," said Jonathan.

"How?" asked Sarah.

"Do you have a mobile phone?" he asked, an idea popping into his head.

Back in London, Jeffrey Petersen, the Deputy Prime Minister was preparing for the meeting with Heron Construction. He sat back and pondered over Jonathan's sudden and strange decision to award the contract to Heron. It had taken Jeffrey by surprise. Up until yesterday, Jonathan had been dead set against Heron Construction, but now he seemed to be their biggest fan. It was so unlike Jonathan – in fact, his decision was bizarre!

It wasn't the only strange thing about Jonathan over the past few days. Jeffrey had noticed that he was behaving oddly, too. He seemed somehow exaggerated and not his usual self. More worryingly, over the last day or two there had been situations where he seemed to have had a complete memory lapse – he was vague about things they'd spoken about before and sometimes he didn't appear to know what he was doing. Jonathan had certainly been under a lot of stress for a while. But over the last couple of days, Jeffrey had started to worry that it was getting to him.

Jeffrey's mobile phone began to ring. He answered it as he slipped on his jacket and headed out of the door to the contract signing.

"Jeffrey, it's Jonathan," said the voice on the phone.

"I'm just on the way to the meeting, Jonathan. Shall we talk then?" said Jeffrey.

"Jeffrey, I know this is going to sound crazy, but I'm in a field somewhere outside London...Hampshire I think," said Jonathan, awkwardly.

Jonathan sounded agitated, thought Jeffrey. He had to calm him down. "Jonathan, you're mistaken. You're in 10 Downing Street. We're about to go to the same meeting," said Jeffrey.

"I'm not in Downing Street, but somebody else is. An impostor who's pretending to be me!" cried Jonathan, desperately.

Jeffrey sighed. This was so weird that it had to be a prank call. "Let me just stop you there," he said, angrily. "I don't know who you are, but pretending to be the Prime Minister will get you into serious trouble. If you don't hang up, I'll have you arrested."

"Jeffrey, I'm telling you the truth! Rufus Heron kidnapped me two days ago," said Jonathan.

"I can have this number traced in an instant," warned Jeffrey.

"A-X-27-B, codeword Eagle," came Jonathan's immediate reply.

Jeffrey froze when he heard those words. It couldn't be, it just couldn't! That was one of the missile codes – it was top secret! So secret, in fact, that only two people in the world knew it – Jeffrey Peterson and Jonathan Holmes.

"Jon?" queried Jeffrey incredulously, his voice trembling with the realisation that it really was the Prime Minister that he was speaking to.

"Yes, Jeffrey, it's me. We have to stop that contract signing! I'm on my way, but you have to delay things for me – buy us some time," said Jonathan, quickly.

"Will do," said Jeffrey, wondering what on earth was going on.

"Thanks, Jeffrey, I'm counting on you!" said Jonathan, relieved that he'd finally been believed.

With that he hung up, leaving Jeffrey to contemplate the very strange situation that he was in. Could it really be true? Was a fake Prime Minister moments away from giving billions of pounds to a criminal? If so, Jeffrey was the only thing standing in the way of that happening! What was he going to do?

Back in the field, Sarah and Jonathan had an equally tricky problem – they were still miles away from London, with no way of getting to the meeting.

"There's only so long Jeffrey can delay things," said Jonathan. "We have to get to Downing Street as fast as we can," he added.

"Leave that to me..." said Sarah, taking her phone and dialling.

Back at M.I.Five HQ, Julian had assembled a group of MI6 agents to track Sarah down. In his usual, cautious way he had a created a detailed plan to locate her and return her to HQ. It was a good plan, he thought, but he hadn't banked on one thing – Sarah was about to do the job for him!

"Excuse me," he said, as his phone began ringing in his pocket. He spluttered with surprise as he saw 'Sarah' flash up on the screen.

"I'm turning myself in," said Sarah as soon as Julian answered.

"Well, I'm very glad you've seen sense. We'll expect you ba…"

"No, Julian. I'm going to set off my tracking beacon so you can find me and pick me up by helicopter."

"Sarah, helicopter fuel is far too expens…"

"That's the deal. You have thirty minutes to get here or I'm off!" she said, hanging up.

Julian sighed loudly and picked up the phone. "Get me a helicopter – right away!" he barked.

Not very far away, inside Number 10 Downing Street, Jeffrey was knocking on the door of the Prime Minister's office. "Come in," called Henry from inside.

Jeffrey entered, carrying a very bulky file. "Sorry to interrupt, Prime Minister, but we need to discuss some urgent matters."

"Does it have to be now? We've got a very important meeting with Mr Heron in five minutes," said Henry, shifting uncomfortably.

As Jeffrey approached the desk, he glanced into

the waste paper basket and noticed a scrunched up piece of paper with nothing but the Prime Minister's signature on it. It was further proof that the voice on the phone was Jonathan. After all, no one needed to practise a signature – unless it wasn't their own. Any remaining doubt that Jeffrey had had was now gone. The man at the desk was an impostor and Jeffrey had to keep him away from that contract!

Jeffrey forced a smile. "I'm afraid there are a few policy issues that need to be discussed in depth before the Heron meeting, Prime Minister."

"What issues?" asked Henry, with concern in his voice. He didn't like talking about things in too much detail – there was always a risk of being caught out.

"No need to worry, Prime Minister," said Jeffrey, taking a seat at the desk and plonking the thick file down with a thump. "You know these policies inside out, so it shouldn't take too long," he added, brightly, as he opened the document at page one.

Meanwhile, Julian and the helicopter pilot were homing in on Sarah's signal. "I think that's her down there!" shouted Julian to the pilot.

"Who's that with her?" asked the pilot, curiously.

"What?" said Julian, taking a closer look. The pilot was right. There were two figures waving up at him. "I've got no idea," he added, crossly.

The helicopter touched down and Julian jumped out, "You've got a lot of explai..." Julian trailed off as he realised that the man standing next to Sarah was none other than Jonathan Holmes, the Prime Minister.

"Julian, in future, I think you'd better listen more carefully to your agents," said Jonathan, frowning.

"Sir, I'm so sorr..." spluttered Julian.

"Never mind all that, we've got work to do. We have to stop Heron signing that contract," said Jonathan.

Julian nodded and, flipping open his mobile, shouted, "Code red! Downing Street!"

Back in the Prime Minister's office, Henry was struggling to keep his eyes open as Jeffrey continued to drone on. "The next thing I wanted to discuss was fishing quotas," said Jeffrey desperately. There was only so long he could keep this up.

"Fishing quotas?" said Henry, looking worried.

"Yes, Prime Minister, as you know recent legislation significantly reduced the..."

Henry stood up. He'd had enough. "I'm sorry Jeffrey, but we're almost half an hour late for the Future Cities meeting. We'll talk fish later!" However, as he opened the door he found his way barred by two stern-faced men in suits.

"I'm sorry, Prime Minister, but you have to stay here, we have orders to arrest you!" said one of the men as they walked into the room.

Henry's face fell; he knew he'd been caught. The realisation that he was going to jail was too much for him and he immediately began blubbing, "I'm s-s-s-sorry, Heron made me d-do it!" he sobbed, slipping back into his own voice.

At that moment, Heron appeared at the door. "Prime Minister, is there a prob..." he trailed off when he noticed the men and the tears streaming down Henry's face. "Never mind," he added, turning on his heel and hurrying away.

"He's in on it, too!" said Jeffrey to the men, as one of them headed after him.

Heron dashed towards the end of the hall where Sue, the Prime Minister's assistant, was standing in the doorway. She watched Heron running towards her, chased by the MI6 agent.

"Move!" he spat.

Sue stepped gracefully aside, but as Heron passed, she stuck her leg out. He fell heavily over her foot, face first on to the floor. Seconds later the MI6 agent caught up with him.

"You're under arrest, Heron," said the agent, slipping handcuffs on to his wrists. "Thanks," he added, to Sue.

"My pleasure," she replied, smiling. "I've never liked him."

Now continue to page 188

robert Has a Trick up His Sleeve

As soon as the drama of Sarah's escape was over, the rest of the kids were bundled into a van and driven to a nearby police station, where their belongings were taken and they were placed in a small cell. Sitting crammed together on the narrow bench, they contemplated the signing of the Heron contract by the fake Prime Minister. Could Sarah really stop it from going ahead?

"She might pull it off," said Jake, hopefully.

"But what if she doesn't?" said Alex, frowning.

"Then we're in big trouble," responded Chun Mai, as she slumped against the wall.

What none of them had noticed was that Robert wasn't paying any attention to their gloomy chatter. He was sitting at the end of the bench, calmly shuffling a deck of cards.

Finally, Chun Mai noticed what he was doing.

"Robert, where did you get those cards from?" she demanded.

"I've got loads of pockets sewn into this jacket for my magic tricks, Chun Mai. They didn't notice," he said, with a wink.

"Well, I don't think this is really the time for card games, do you?" said Jake, crossly.

"Let's see if you still feel that way in a few minutes," retorted Robert, walking over to the door.

"What do you mean?" asked Alex.

"You'll see," said Robert, before shouting for the guard at the top of his voice.

The rest of the kids looked at each other in confusion. Before long, a policeman showed up at the door of their cell.

"What do you want?" he demanded.

"I'm sorry, but I forgot to hand in all of my possessions earlier," said Robert. "I still have a deck of cards here."

There was a deep sigh from the policeman and after a moment the lock clicked as he opened the door and stepped into the cell, "Hand 'em over then," he said, holding out his hand.

"How about a trick first?" said Robert.

"No. It's against procedure," responded the policeman, firmly.

"Please, just one. I promise we'll be on our best behaviour for the rest of our stay," wheedled Robert.

"Oh, for heaven's sake. Okay, but make it fast," said the policeman, folding his arms.

Robert smiled and fanned the cards out. "Pick a card," he said. The policeman picked a card and looked at it. "Now put it back," instructed Robert. The guard slipped the card back in the middle of the deck.

Robert sighed and placed the deck of cards on to the bench, folding his arms haughtily. "Well, if you're not going to play by the rules, then there's no point!" he said with mock outrage.

"What're you talking about?" said the policeman.

"I asked you to put the card back in the deck," replied Robert, pretending to be irritated.

"I did!" exclaimed the policeman.

"No you didn't. It's in your pocket," said Robert, as he reached into the policeman's pocket and pulled out the ace of diamonds. "That is your card, right?"

"Yes..." said the policeman, with surprise. "How did you do that?"

"Magic," said Robert. "Why don't you get your mate and see if we can bamboozle him?" he said, pointing to another policeman further along the corridor.

"Okay," said the policeman. "Fred! Come and see this!" he called to the other policeman.

Fred hurried in, "What's up?" he said, in concern.

"Nothing, mate. You just gotta see this trick, that's all!" he said, getting Robert to repeat it.

As Robert took the eight of hearts out of Fred's

pocket, the policemen both shook their heads. "Well I never," said the first one. "Well, you've certainly brightened up my day! Show us another," he said.

"No, it's against procedure. I don't want to get you in trouble," said Robert, handing over the deck.

The policemen smiled as they left the cell, discussing how they thought it was done, as the first policeman locked the door behind them.

"And what was the point of that?" demanded Chun Mai. "This is hardly the time to show off!"

Robert simply smiled and dangled a set of keys in front of her face. "The eight of hearts wasn't all I took out of Fred's pocket," he replied, smugly. The kids began to shout congratulations but Robert frantically gestured for them to be quiet. "Shh! We have to be careful or we'll be found out!"

Robert put the key into the door as quietly as he could, and slowly turned it. He gently swung the door open and crept into the corridor, followed slowly and silently by the rest of the kids. They tip-toed to the end of the hall and peeked around the corner. Their path was blocked by the same policeman Robert had tricked a moment ago. He was sitting behind the front desk, blocking the way to the front door.

"So, how are we going to get out of here?" whispered Chun Mai.

Fred was engrossed. He was playing with Robert's deck of cards, trying to work out how the trick had been done. Despite his newfound interest, he would probably notice four kids running past him. They needed a plan.

"I have an idea," said Jake, pointing to Alex's shoes – as ever, his laces were undone. He said, "Alex, bung me a shoelace. Chun Mai, how fast can you run?"

"Why?" asked Chun Mai, suspiciously. She knew this would be another plan she wouldn't like. "And what are you going to do with Alex's lace?"

A few seconds later, the policeman was fed up with the cards. He threw the pack down in frustration. "Stupid cards!" he said crossly, picking up some paperwork.

"Excuse me," said a voice. The policeman looked up and was taken aback to see Chun Mai standing in front of him. "I thought I'd stretch my legs, if that's okay with you?"

He looked at her in complete shock before jumping up to grab her. Chun Mai was too fast, flying down the corridor with the policeman in hot pursuit.

As she rounded a corner, she leapt over the shoelace that Robert and Jake had stretched tightly across the corridor. Fortunately, the policeman wasn't so nimble. He tripped and fell heavily. Alex seized his chance, jumping on to his back and securing the policeman's hands with his own cuffs.

"Let's go," shouted Chun Mai. "Before the other guy comes back!"

"Oi!" yelled the policeman as they fled. "Come back here!"

"Hurry up, Alex," urged Robert, as they ran down the corridor and out of the front door.

"I'm trying!" said Alex. "I've lost a lace – remember?" Chun Mai shook her head and laughed. She wondered why Alex was struggling – his laces were always undone anyway!

Meanwhile, Jonathan was staring at the ground thousands of feet below. He was trying to get his head around the fact that he was in an invisible flying machine, piloted by a twelve-year-old girl.

"We have to get to Downing Street!" said Jonathan. "If we don't make it in the next half an hour the look-alike will disappear and there'll be no way to prove what happened!"

"I'll do my best, Jonathan," said Sarah, as a repetitive bleeping interrupted. Sarah looked at the dashboard and saw a red warning light flashing.

"What does that mean?" asked Jonathan.

"I don't know," admitted Sarah. "I've never flown this thing before!"

Jonathan turned white with fear. He gripped the edge of the seat so hard that he was in danger of tearing the fabric. Unfortunately, Sarah didn't have time to reassure him – her phone was ringing.

"Sorry, Prime Minister," she said, answering the phone. "Hello?"

The rest of the kids had piled into a phone box about half a mile away from the police station. "Sarah, it's me," said Jake.

"Jake! But how..." began Sarah.

"We're fine. We've escaped. How're you getting on?" he interrupted.

"I've found the Prime Minister! We're somewhere above Europe in the hoverpod," she said, proudly.

"She's found him!" said Jake to the rest of the kids, who whooped and high-fived happily.

Sarah glanced at the ominous warning light on the dashboard. "Actually Jake, can I speak to Alex?" she said, suddenly serious.

"Sure," said Jake passing the phone to Alex, which wasn't easy in the packed phone box.

"Alex, what does the red flashing light on the dashboard mean?" asked Sarah, with concern.

"Oh," said Alex.

"What do you mean, 'Oh'?" asked Sarah, starting to get worried.

"It means the engines are overheating," said Alex, urgently. "You have to slow down. Make sure you keep your speed below a hundred miles per hour," he warned.

Sarah glanced nervously at her watch, they wouldn't make it in time if she did that. "What happens if I don't?" she asked.

"It'll all go pear-shaped. Basically, the engines

will blow up and you'll drop down to earth like a stone!" said Alex, simply.

"Oh," said Sarah, slowing the hoverpod down until the speedo was steadily pointing below the hundred mark. "Err, thanks for the safety tip Alex. Can I speak to Jake again?"

Alex passed the phone receiver back across the cramped phone box to Jake.

"Jake, can you think of anything that might delay the contract signing?" she begged.

"Delay the signing? I don't see what we can do, we're on the run from the law!" said Jake.

Just then, Robert began gesticulating wildly. "I've thought of something!" he mouthed, as the pips sounded to signal that their time was running out.

"Robert's got a plan!" blurted Jake.

"Okay, do what you need..." said Sarah as the line went dead.

Jake hung up the phone and the kids burst from the packed phone box on to the pavement. "Well, let's hear your idea, Robert!" said Chun Mai.

Robert fished around in one of his hidden pockets and pulled out a small piece of paper.

"What's that?" asked Alex.

"This is Jack Holmes's phone number," replied Robert, with a smug grin.

"Who's Jack Holmes?" asked Chun Mai.

"The Prime Minister's son," replied Robert.

"Impressive, I guess, but I don't see how having his phone number helps us," said Jake.

"I did a magic show at a royal event last month and Jack was there. We really hit it off, he wants me to teach him some tricks actually," said Robert, airily.

"So?" asked Chun Mai.

"Look, I don't have time to explain every detail to you lot. Somebody give me change for the phone!" said Robert, shortly.

"Well we haven't got any other ideas!" shrugged Jake, as he handed Robert some coins.

Across town, in his bedroom in 10 Downing Street, Jack Holmes was bored. He'd watched TV, played computer games and read books, but nothing could hold his attention for more than a few minutes. Jack let out a deep, frustrated sigh and flopped back on to his bed. Just then, his mobile began to ring. He didn't recognise the number, but he answered it anyway. "Hello...?" he said.

"Jack, hi. It's Robert," said Robert.

"Who?" asked Jack, puzzled.

"You know, The Great Roberto," answered Robert impatiently.

Jack sat up straight. "Oh, yeah, I remember! We met at Buckingham Palace, didn't we? I was hoping you'd call, Robert!"

"Listen, I need your help with something!" said Robert, urgently.

"Is it a magic trick?" asked Jack, curiously, hoping for some tips.

Robert bit his lip. He didn't like the idea of lying to Jack, but this was an unusual situation. "Yes, actually it is!" he said, brightly. "It's my latest illusion. If we do it right, it'll be big news in the world of magic."

"Cool! I'm in," said Jack, excitedly, as he pictured the headlines.

"Good! Now, listen very carefully," said Robert as he outlined his plan to his eager new assistant.

Meanwhile, downstairs in the White Drawing Room, various government ministers and assistants were assembling. Heron and Henry sat together at the end of the table. Unsurprisingly, Heron was in a good mood. In another half an hour the deal would be done. The Future Cities contract would be his and he would have pulled off the greatest illusion in history. Not that he could tell anyone, of course. In contrast, Henry was simply glad that the experience was nearly over. He couldn't wait to get his hands on some much-needed cash.

The Prime Minister's assistant appeared at the door. "Prime Minister? Jack's just called," she said.

"Jack who?" said Henry, looking confused.

"Err...your son?" said Sue, raising an eyebrow.

"Oh, yes of course," said Henry, trying to laugh off the mistake. "Is he okay?"

"No, I'm afraid not, sir. He says he's feeling ill

and he needs you to go and see him."

"I can't at the moment, Sue," said Henry. "I'm in a very important meeting."

The people around the table were a little shocked at the Prime Minister's reaction – it was most unlike him. Jeffrey Petersen, the Deputy Prime Minister, spoke up. "It's okay, Prime Minister. If you would like to take a few minutes to see him, I'm sure everyone would be happy to wait."

"Ahem!" Heron cleared his throat and subtly raised his head to meet Henry's gaze

"No, I really think we should push on!" blustered Henry, noticing that Heron was annoyed.

"Honestly, Prime Minister, it's fine," said another member of the government. "I'm sure Mr Heron won't mind waiting."

"My schedule is quite tight as I do have some other meetings to attend this afternoon," said Heron, calmly. But, noticing the surprised looks on the faces around him, he decided to back off a little. "But nothing that can't wait half an hour," he said, smoothly.

"Very well," said Henry, seeing that he had no choice.

He climbed the stairs and walked along the corridor, suddenly realising that he didn't know where Jack's room was. He'd been avoiding Jonathan's family, as he knew that the people closest to him would be much more difficult to fool. Fortunately for Henry, Jack's door had a sign with his name on it.

"Jack?" he called. "What's wrong, boy?" But there was no reply.

Henry walked into Jack's room but, to his surprise, it was empty. He was about to walk out, when the door suddenly slammed shut behind him and he heard a key turn in the lock. "Hey!" he cried, rushing to the handle and shaking it violently. But it was no use, the door would not open.

Jack ran down the hallway chuckling, as thumping noises and swear-words came from inside his room. He dialled the payphone on his mobile and Robert picked up immediately.

"I did it!" Jack said, gleefully.

"Nice one, mate!" said Robert.

"So, come on, what's the next part of the trick?" asked Jack, eagerly.

"I'll handle that," replied Robert. "Just don't let anybody near your room and, whatever you do, don't open that door!"

By now, the hoverpod had managed to rattle its way back to London, but as the engines started to fall apart, it was getting really tricky to control. Sarah's phone rang. She answered it, wedging it between her ear and her shoulder as she battled to steer. "Tell me some good news," she said.

"Okay, how about this? The fake Prime Minister is locked in Jack Holmes's bedroom," said Robert.

"Brill! How did you manage that?" asked Sarah. She never got to hear the answer, however, as one of the engines finally gave up with a loud, shuddering bang. The hoverpod went into an uncontrollable spin and Sarah braced herself for impact. The machine bounced and skidded its way down Parliament Street, scraping walls and denting lampposts as it went. When it finally came to a halt, Sarah gingerly opened her eyes and looked across at Jonathan. He was as white as a sheet, but apart from a couple of cuts and bruises, he appeared to be okay.

As they clambered out, Sarah noticed with a smile that they were right outside the entrance to Downing Street. "That was lucky," she grinned.

"In more ways than one," added Jonathan. He was very relieved to be back on the ground.

The guard at the entrance to Downing Street looked absolutely flabbergasted as he opened the gate for the Prime Minister. "If anyone asks, tell them it's a car," said Sarah, pointing at the wrecked hoverpod as they rushed in.

Back in the White Drawing room, Heron was getting twitchy. He couldn't shake the feeling that something was up; that his plans were going to unravel at the last minute. "I hope the Prime Minister's son is okay," he said, coolly. "He's certainly been gone a while."

"I'm back now!" said Jonathan Holmes, as he burst through the door, accompanied by Sarah and two policemen. The MPs gasped as they looked at their Prime Minister. How had he got so bruised and

dishevelled? What on earth had gone on in Jack's room they wondered? "Arrest him, officers," said Jonathan, pointing at Heron.

"What's this all about?" asked Heron anxiously, as the policemen bundled him out of the door. "This is an outrage! I'm an honest businessman. I'll sue!" he cried, as he was dragged down the hall.

"When you're done with him, you can arrest the man who is currently locked in my son's room for impersonating me!" commanded Jonathan.

Jonathan turned to face the stunned members of parliament standing before him. Each one of them was open-mouthed in shock.

"Prime Minister?" said Jeffrey. "Would you mind explaining what's been going on?"

"All in due course, Jeffrey," replied Jonathan. "There's something I need to do first," he added, picking up the Heron contract. With one swift movement he tore it in half and breathed a deep sigh of relief as the pieces fluttered to the floor.

Sarah smiled. Mission accomplished!

Now turn the page...

12
THE NEXT DAY

The next day, Downing Street had returned to its usual state of relative calm as the real Prime Minister returned to running the country. The kids were all given full apologies and reinstated as agents immediately. They were keen to get back to work, but before they did, the Prime Minister had asked to see them.

"I still can't believe you actually did it!" said Jake to Sarah, as they waited nervously in Jonathan's office.

"We did it," said Sarah, correcting Jake. "I just handled the last bit."

"Even so, nice work," said Chun Mai, smiling at her friend.

"Ah, my favourite secret agents," said Jonathan, as he breezed through the office door, looking refreshed after a bath and a good night's sleep. He shook each of the kids warmly by the hand. "You'll be delighted to know that Rufus Heron and my look-alike, Henry Allinson, have been charged. It looks as if they'll be going to prison for a very long time."

"What about Snidley?" asked Sarah.

"Snidley will be joining them. The French police arrested him on The Billionaire" he smiled. Then Jonathan looked serious for a moment. "If it hadn't been for you guys, Heron would've got that contract. We would all have been in deep trouble. There must be something I can do to thank you…"

Robert piped up immediately. "Actually, Prime Minister, now you mention it, I could do with a…"

"We don't need anything, thank you," interrupted Sarah, shooting Robert a fierce look. "We're just glad that you're back in one piece and that Heron's behind bars."

Jonathan smiled. "Very well, although I think there's at least one person who owes you an apology." He pressed the intercom and said, "Send him in, Sue."

The door swung open and Julian stood in the doorway looking very sheepish. "Prime Minister, I am delighted to see you're back safe and sound."

"Thank you, Julian, but that's really down to the M.I.Five here," said Jonathan.

"Yes, of course it is," said Julian, "Agents, I apologise – I underestimated you all," said Julian, clearing his throat.

"Don't mention it, Julian," said Chun Mai.

"Julian is being moved to a different department

in MI6," said Jonathan. "I think he'll be better suited elsewhere."

Julian nodded, but it was clear that he wasn't happy about the move.

"Umm, actually, Sir," said Jake. "I have to respectfully disagree with you there."

"What do you mean?" asked Jonathan, intrigued.

"I think Julian has been a pretty good boss, actually," said Jake tentatively – disagreeing with the most powerful man in the country was not an easy thing to do.

"When we disobeyed orders, he put his neck on the line with the big wigs. He promised them he'd sort us out," Jake continued as Julian looked at him in shock, with his eyebrows raised – he hadn't expected anyone to stick up for him.

"He had no choice but to send us to the cells when we defied him again. He thought he was doing the right thing. He's a great agent and I think he reins us in when we get a bit...well...over enthusiastic. To be honest, there's no one I'd rather learn from."

When Jake had finished talking, Julian did something that none of the other kids had ever seen him do – he actually smiled.

"Do you all feel this way?" asked Jonathan. All the kids nodded, "Well then, I can't very well disagree, can I? Julian, consider yourself reinstated as the commanding officer of the M.I.Five! I'll clear it with your bosses – if you still want the job?"

"Of course I do, Prime Minister. Thank you guys," said Julian, turning to the M.I.Five and nodding in appreciation.

"Very good," said Jonathan. "Now, there was one more thing. If you wouldn't mind turning your attention to the screen on that wall over there," he said, pointing. The kids turned to face a screen displaying a plan of a city.

"What's that, Prime Minister?" asked Sarah.

"That is Sir Brian Wilkins' plan for his first Future City," replied Jonathan. The kids rushed over to the screen to get a better look. "Well, actually, that's the updated plan," he continued. "I called Sir Brian this morning and asked for some changes."

"What kind of changes?" asked Sarah.

"Wow! Look! There's a street called Chun Mai Drive!" said Chun Mai leaping about in excitement.

"Let's just say some of the roads are now named after some of my favourite people," grinned Jonathan.

"There's Robert Road," said Robert. "Look, Chun Mai, my road's bigger than yours," he goaded, with a wicked grin.

"And there's Jake Gardens," cried Jake, excitedly.

"There's mine. Look – Alex Avenue!" said Alex, looking really pleased.

"Of course, everything that happened with Rufus

Heron is top secret," said Julian, settling back into his position of authority. "So you won't be able to tell anybody that the streets are named after you."

"We'll know, though," said Jake, proudly. "And that's good enough for me!"

Sarah began to frown slightly; she had scanned the whole map, but couldn't see her name anywhere.

"Don't worry, Sarah," said Jonathan, with a smile. "I haven't forgotten you. Take a look at the top of the screen."

Somewhat confused, Sarah glanced upwards and gasped with surprise and delight. The biggest smile her friends had ever seen stretched across her face as she read the name of the new city. It was called 'Sarahville'.

"Wow," said Sarah, overcome with pride.

"In recognition of a job well done," said Jonathan. "Thank you, Sarah, for all your determination and bravery – you're truly remarkable."

M.I.Five